BRAIN TWISTER

FINE SCIENCE FICTION AND FANTASY TITLES AVAILABLE FROM CARROLL & GRAF

☐ Aldiss, Brian/THE DARK LIGHT YEARS	$3.50
☐ Aldiss, Brian/LAST ORDERS	$3.50
☐ Aldiss, Brian/NON-STOP	$3.95
☐ Amis, Kingsley/THE ALTERATION	$3.50
☐ Asimov, Isaac et al. (eds)/THE MAMMOTH BOOK OF VINTAGE SCIENCE FICTION (1950s)	$8.95
☐ Asimov, Isaac et al/THE MAMMOTH BOOK OF GOLDEN AGE SCIENCE FICTION (1940s)	$8.95
☐ Ballard, J.G./THE DROWNED WORLD	$3.95
☐ Ballard, J.G./THE TERMINAL BEACH	$3.50
☐ Ballard, J.G./VERMILION SANDS	$3.95
☐ Bingley, Margaret/SEEDS OF EVIL	$3.95
☐ Borges, Jorge Luis/THE BOOK OF FANTASY (Trade Paper)	$10.95
☐ Boucher, Anthony/THE COMPLEAT WEREWOLF	$4.50
☐ Campbell, John W./THE MOON IS HELL!	$3.95
☐ Campbell, Ramsey/DEMONS BY DAYLIGHT	$3.95
☐ Burroughs, Edgar Rice/A PRINCESS OF MARS	$2.95
☐ Dick, Philip K./THE PENULTIMATE TRUTH	$3.95
☐ Dick, Philip K./TIME OUT OF JOINT	$3.95
☐ Disch, Thomas K./CAMP CONCENTRATION	$3.95
☐ Leiber, Fritz/YOU'RE ALL ALONE	$3.95
☐ Leinster, Murray/THE FORGOTTEN PLANET	$3.95
☐ Ligotti, Thomas/SONGS OF A DEAD DREAMER	$3.95
☐ Lovecraft, H. P. & Derleth, A./THE LURKER ON THE THRESHOLD	$3.50
☐ Moorcock, Michael/FANTASY: THE 100 BEST BOOKS	$8.95
☐ Stoker, Bram/THE JEWEL OF SEVEN STARS	$3.95
☐ van Vogt, A.E./COSMIC ENCOUNTER	$3.50
☐ Watson, Ian/CHEKHOV'S JOURNEY	$3.95
☐ Watson, Ian/MIRACLE VISITORS	$3.95

Available from fine bookstores everywhere or use this coupon for ordering.

Carroll & Graf Publishers, Inc., 260 Fifth Avenue, N.Y., N.Y. 10001

Please send me the books I have checked above. I am enclosing $_____ (please add $1.25 per title to cover postage and handling.) Send check or money order—no cash or C.O.D.'s please. N.Y. residents please add 8¼% sales tax.

Mr/Mrs/Ms _____
Address _____
City _____ State/Zip _____
Please allow four to six weeks for delivery.

BRAIN TWISTER

**RANDALL GARRETT
& LAURENCE M. JANIFER**

Carroll & Graf Publishers, Inc.
New York

Copyright © 1962 by Pyramid Publications, Inc.

All rights reserved

Published by arrangement with the Scott Meredith Literary Agency, Inc.

First Carroll & Graf edition 1992

Carroll & Graf Publishers, Inc.
260 Fifth Avenue
New York, NY 10001

ISBN: 0-88184-845-X

Manufactured in the United States of America

A shorter version of this work appeared in *Astounding Science Fiction* under the title of *That Sweet Little Old Lady*.

PROLOGUE

In nineteen-fourteen, it was enemy aliens.

In nineteen-thirty, it was Wobblies.

In nineteen-fifty-seven, it was fellow-travelers.

And, in nineteen seventy-one, Kenneth J. Malone rolled wearily out of bed wondering what the hell it was going to be now.

One thing, he told himself, was absolutely certain: it was going to be terrible. It always was.

He managed to stand up, although he was swaying slightly when he walked across the room to the mirror for his usual morning look at himself. He didn't much like staring at his own face, first thing in the morning, but then, he told himself, it was part of the toughening-up process every FBI agent had to go through. You had to learn to stand up and take it when things got rough, he reminded himself. He blinked and looked into the mirror.

His image blinked back.

He tried a smile. It looked pretty horrible, he thought —but, then, the mirror had a slight ripple in it, and the ripple distorted everything. Malone's face looked as if it had been gently patted with a waffle-iron.

And, of course, it was still early morning, and that meant he was having a little difficulty in focusing his eyes.

Vaguely, he tried to remember the night before. He was just ending his vacation, and he thought he recalled having a final farewell party for two or three lovely female types he had chanced to meet in what was still the world's finest City of Opportunity, Washington, D.C. (latest female-to-male ratio, five-and-a-half to one). The party had been a classic of its kind, complete with hot and cold running ideas of all sorts, and lots and lots of nice powerful liquor.

Malone decided sadly that the ripple wasn't in the mirror, but in his head. He stared at his unshaven face blearily.

Blink.

Ripple.

Quite impossible, he told himself. Nobody could conceivably look as horrible as Kenneth J. Malone thought he did. Things just couldn't be as bad as all that.

Ignoring a still, small voice which asked persistently: "Why not?" he turned away from the mirror and set about finding his clothes. He determined to take his time about getting ready for work: after all, nobody could really complain if he arrived late on his first day after vacation. Everybody knew how tired vacations made a person.

And, besides, there was probably nothing happening anyway. Things had, he recalled with faint pleasure, been pretty quiet lately. Ever since the counterfeiting gang he'd caught had been put away, crime seemed to have dropped to the nice, simple levels of the 1950's and '60's. Maybe, he hoped suddenly, he'd be able to spend some time catching up on his scientific techniques, or his math, or pistol practice. . . .

The thought of pistol practice made his head begin to throb with the authority of a true hangover. There were fifty or sixty small gnomes inside his skull, he realized, all of them with tiny little hammers. They were mining for lead.

"The lead," Malone said aloud, "is farther down. Not in the skull."

The gnomes paid him no attention. He shut his eyes and tried to relax. The gnomes went right ahead with their work, and microscopic regiments of Eagle Scouts began marching steadily along his nerves.

There were people, Malone had always understood, who bounced out of their beds and greeted each new day with a smile. It didn't sound possible, but then again there were some pretty strange people. The head of that counterfeiting ring, for instance: where had he got the idea of picking an alias like André Gide?

Clutching at his whirling thoughts, Malone opened his eyes, winced, and began to get dressed. At least, he thought, it was going to be a peaceful day.

It was at this second that his private intercom buzzed.

Malone winced again. "To hell with you," he called at the thing, but the buzz went on, ignoring the code shut-off. That meant, he knew, an emergency call, maybe from his Chief of Section. Maybe even from higher up.

"I'm not even late for work yet," he complained. "I will be, but I'm not yet. What are they screaming about?"

There was, of course, only one way to find out. He shuffled painfully across the room, flipped the switch and said:

"Malone here." Vaguely, he wondered if it were true. He certainly didn't feel as if he were here. Or there. Or anywhere at all, in fact.

A familiar voice came tinnily out of the receiver. "Malone, get down here right away!"

The voice belonged to Andrew J. Burris. Malone sighed deeply and felt grateful, for the fiftieth time, that he had never had a TV pickup installed in the intercom. He didn't want the FBI chief to see him looking as horrible as he did now, all rippled and everything. It wasn't—well, it wasn't professional, that was all.

"I'll get dressed right away," he assured the intercom. "I should be there in—"

"Don't bother to get dressed," Burris snapped. "This is an emergency!"

"But, Chief—"

"And don't call me Chief!"

"Okay," Malone said. "Sure. You want me to come down in my pyjamas. Right?"

"I want you to—" Burris stopped. "All right, Malone. If you want to waste time while our country's life is at stake, you go ahead. Get dressed. After all, Malone, when I say something is an emergency—"

"I won't get dressed, then," Malone said. "Whatever you say."

"Just do something!" Burris told him desperately. "Your country needs you. Pyjamas and all. Malone, it's a crisis!"

Conversations with Burris, Malone told himself, were bound to be a little confusing. "I'll be right down," he said.

"Fine," Burris said, and hesitated. Then he added: "Malone, do you wear the tops or the bottoms?"

"The what?"

"Of your pyjamas," Burris explained hurriedly. "The top part or the bottom part?"

"Oh," Malone said. "As a matter of fact, I wear both."

"Good," Burris said with satisfaction. "I wouldn't want an agent of mine arrested for indecent exposure." He rang off.

Malone blinked at the intercom for a minute, shut it off and then, ignoring the trip-hammers in his skull and the Eagle Scouts on his nerves, began to get dressed. Somehow, in spite of Burris' feelings of crisis, he couldn't see himself tying to flag a taxi on the streets of Washington in his pyjamas. Anyhow, not while he was awake.

I dreamed I was an FBI agent, he thought sadly, in my drafty BVDs.

Besides, it was probably nothing important. These

things, he told himself severely, have a way of evaporating as soon as a clear, cold intelligence got hold of them.

Then he began wondering where in hell he was going to find a clear, cold intelligence. Or even, for that matter, what one was.

1

"They could be anywhere," Burris said, with an expression which bordered on exasperated horror. "They could be all around us. Heaven only knows."

He pushed his chair back from his desk and stood up, a chunky little man with bright blue eyes and large hands. He paced to the window and looked out at Washington, and then he came back to the desk. A persistent office rumor held that he had become head of the FBI purely because he happened to have an initial *J* in his name, but in his case the *J* stood for Jeremiah. And, at the moment, his tone expressed all the hopelessness of that Old Testament prophet's lamentations.

"We're helpless," he said, looking at the young man with the crisp brown hair who was sitting across the desk. "That's what it is, we're helpless."

Kenneth Malone tried to look dependable. "Just tell me what to do," he said.

"You're a good agent, Kenneth," Burris said. "You're one of the best. That's why you've been picked for this job. And I want to say that I picked you personally. Believe me, there's never been anything like it before."

"I'll do my best," Malone said at random. He was twenty-six, and he had been an FBI agent for three years. In that time, he had, among other things, managed to break up a gang of smugglers, track down a counterfeiting ring, and capture three kidnappers. For reasons which he could neither understand nor explain, no one seemed willing to attribute his record to luck.

"I know you will," Burris said. "And if anybody can crack this case, Malone, you're the man. It's just that —everything sounds so *impossible*. Even after all the conferences we've had."

"Conferences?" Malone said vaguely. He wished the Chief would get to the point. Any point. He smiled gently across the desk and tried to look competent and dependable and reassuring. Burris' expression didn't change.

"You'll get the conference tapes later," Burris said. "You can study them before you leave. I suggest you study them very carefully, Malone. Don't be like me. Don't get confused." He buried his face in his hands. Malone waited patiently. After a few seconds, Burris looked up. "Did you read books when you were a child?" he asked.

Malone said: "What?"

"Books," Burris said. "When you were a child. Read them."

"Sure I did," Malone said. "*Bomba the Jungle Boy,* and *Doctor Doolittle,* and *Lucky Starr,* and *Little Women*—"

"*Little Women?*"

"When Beth died," Malone said, "I wanted to cry. But I didn't. My father said big boys don't cry."

"And your father was right," Burris said. "Why, when I was a—never mind. Forget about Beth and your father. Think about Lucky Starr for a minute. Remember him?"

"Sure," Malone said. "I liked those books. You know it's funny, but the books you read when you're a kid, they kind of stay with you. Know what I mean? I can still remember that one about Venus, for instance. Gee, that was—"

"Never mind about Venus, too," Burris said sharply. "Keep your mind on the problem."

"Yes, sir," Malone said. He paused. "What problem, sir?" he added.

"The problem we're discussing," Burris said. He gave Malone a bright, blank stare. "My God," he said. "Just listen to me."

"Yes, sir."

"All right, then." Burris took a deep breath. He seemed nervous. Once again he stood up and went to the window. This time, he spoke without turning. "Remember how everybody used to laugh about spaceships, and orbital satellites, and life on other planets? That was just in those Lucky Starr books. That was all just for kids, wasn't it?"

"Well, I don't know," Malone said slowly.

"Sure it was all for kids," Burris said. "It was laughable. Nobody took it seriously."

"Well, *somebody* must—"

"You just keep quiet and listen," Burris said.

"Yes, sir," Malone said.

Burris nodded. His hands were clasped behind his back. "We're not laughing any more, are we, Malone?" he said without moving.

There was silence.

"Well, are we?"

"Did you want me to answer, sir?"

"Of course I did!" Burris snapped.

"You told me to keep quiet and—"

"Never mind what I told you," Burris said. "Just do what I told you."

"Yes, sir," Malone said. "No, sir," he added after a second.

13

"No, sir, what?" Burris asked softly.

"No, sir, we're not laughing any more," Malone said.

"Ah," Burris said. "And why aren't we laughing any more?"

There was a little pause. Malone said, tentatively: "Because there's nothing to laugh about, sir?"

Burris whirled. "On the head!" he said happily. "You've hit the nail on the head, Kenneth. I knew I could depend on you." His voice grew serious again, and thoughtful. "We're not laughing any more because there's nothing to laugh about. We have orbital satellites, and we've landed on the Moon with an atomic rocket. The planets are the next step, and after that the stars. Man's heritage, Kenneth. The stars. And the stars, Kenneth, belong to Man—not to the Russians!"

"Yes, sir," Malone said soberly.

"So," Burris said, "we should learn not to laugh any more. But have we?"

"I don't know, sir."

"We haven't," Burris said with decision. "Can you read my mind?"

"No, sir," Malone said.

"Can I read your mind?"

Malone hesitated. At last he said: "Not that I know of, sir."

"Well, I can't," Burris snapped. "And can any of us read each other's mind?"

Malone shook his head. "No, sir," he said.

Burris nodded. "That's the problem," he said. "That's the case I'm sending you out to crack."

This time, the silence was a long one.

At last, Malone said: "What problem, sir?"

"Mind reading," Burris said. "There's a spy at work in the Nevada plant, Kenneth. And the spy is a telepath."

The video tapes were very clear and very complete. There were a great many of them, and it was long after nine o'clock when Kenneth Malone decided to take a break and get some fresh air. Washington was a good city for walking, even at night, and Malone liked to walk. Sometimes he pretended, even to himself, that he got his best ideas while walking, but he knew perfectly well that wasn't true. His best ideas just seemed to come to him, out of nowhere, precisely as the situation demanded them.

He was just lucky, that was all. He had a talent for being lucky. But nobody would ever believe that. A record like his was spectacular, even in the annals of the FBI, and Burris himself believed that the record showed some kind of superior ability.

Malone knew that wasn't true, but what could he do about it? After all, he didn't want to resign, did he? It was kind of romantic and exciting to be an FBI agent, even after three years. A man got a chance to travel around a lot and see things, and it was interesting. The pay was pretty good, too.

The only trouble was that, if he didn't quit, he was going to have to find a telepath.

The notion of telepathic spies just didn't sound right to Malone. It bothered him in a remote sort of way. Not that the idea of telepathy itself was alien to him—after all, he was even more aware than the average citizen that research had been going on in that field for something over a quarter of a century, and that the research was even speeding up.

But the cold fact that a telepathy-detecting device had been invented somehow shocked his sense of propriety, and his notions of privacy. It wasn't decent, that was all.

There ought to be something sacred, he told himself angrily.

He stopped walking and looked up. He was on Pennsylvania Avenue, heading toward the White House.

That was no good. He went to the corner and turned off, down the block. He had, he told himself, nothing at all to see the President about.

Not yet, anyhow.

The streets were dark and very peaceful. *I get my best ideas while walking,* Malone said without convincing himself. He thought back to the video tapes.

The report on the original use of the machine itself had been on one of the first tapes, and Malone could still see and hear it. That was one thing he did have, he reflected; his memory was pretty good.

Burris had been the first speaker on the tapes, and he'd given the serial and reference number in a cold, matter-of-fact voice. His face had been perfectly blank, and he looked just like the head of the FBI people were accustomed to seeing on their TV and newsreel screens. Malone wondered what had happened to him between the time the tapes had been made and the time he'd sent for Malone.

Maybe the whole notion of telepathy was beginning to get him, Malone thought.

Burris recited the standard tape-opening in a rapid mumble, like a priest involved in the formula of the Mass: "Any person or agent unauthorized for this tape please refrain from viewing further, under penalties as prescribed by law." Then he looked off, out past the screen to the left, and said: "Dr. Thomas O'Connor, of Westinghouse Laboratories. Will you come here, Dr. O'Connor?"

Dr. O'Connor came into the lighted square of screen slowly, looking all around him. "This is very fascinating," he said, blinking in the lamplight. "I hadn't realized that you people took so many precautions—"

He was, Malone thought, somewhere between fifty and sixty, tall and thin with skin so transparent that he nearly looked like a living X-ray. He had pale blue eyes and pale white hair, and, Malone thought, if there ever were a contest for the best-looking ghost, Dr. Thomas O'Connor would win it hands (or phalanges) down.

"This is all necessary for the national security," Burris said, a little sternly.

"Oh," Dr. O'Connor said quickly. "I realize that, of course. Naturally. I can certainly see that."

"Let's go ahead, shall we?" Burris said.

O'Connor nodded. "Certainly. Certainly."

Burris said: "Well, then," and paused. After a second he started again: "Now, Dr. O'Connor, would you please give us a sort of verbal run-down on this for our records?"

"Of course," Dr. O'Connor said. He smiled into the

video cameras and cleared his throat. "I take it you don't want an explanation of how this machine works. I mean: you don't want a technical exposition, do you?"

"No," Burris said, and added: "Not by any means. Just tell us what it does."

Dr. O'Connor suddenly reminded Malone of a professor he'd had in college for one of the law courses. He had, Malone thought, the same smiling gravity of demeanor, the same condescending attitude of absolute authority. It was clear that Dr. O'Connor lived in a world of his own, a world that was not even touched by the common run of men.

"Well," he began, "to put it very simply, the device indicates whether or not a man's mental—ah—processes are being influenced by outside—by outside influences." He gave the cameras another little smile. "If you will allow me, I will demonstrate on the machine itself."

He took two steps that carried him out of camera range, and returned wheeling a large heavy-looking box. Dangling from the metal covering were a number of wires and attachments. A long cord led from the box to the floor. and snaked out of sight to the left.

"Now," Dr. O'Connor said. He selected a single lead, apparently, Malone thought, at random. "This electrode—"

"Just a moment, Doctor," Burris said. He was eyeing the machine with a combination of suspicion and awe. "A while back you mentioned something about 'outside influences.' Just what, specifically, does that mean?"

With some regret, Dr. O'Connor dropped the lead. "Telepathy," he said. "By outside influences, I meant influences on the mind, such as telepathy or mind-reading of some nature."

"I see," Burris said. "You can detect a telepath with this machine."

"I'm afraid—"

"Well, some kind of a mind-reader anyhow," Burris said. "We won't quarrel about terms."

"Certainly not," Dr. O'Connor said. The smile he turned on Burris was as cold and empty as the inside of Orbital Station One. "What I meant was—if you will permit me to continue—that we cannot detect any sort of telepathy or mind-reader with this device. To be frank, I very much wish that we could; it would make everything a great deal simpler. However, the laws of psionics don't seem to operate that way."

"Well, then," Burris said, "what does the thing do?" His face wore a mask of confusion. Momentarily, Malone felt sorry for his chief. He could remember how he'd felt, himself, when that law professor had come up with a particularly baffling question in class.

"This machine," Dr. O'Connor said with authority, "detects the slight variations in mental activity that occur when a person's mind is *being* read."

"You mean, if my mind were being read right now—"

"Not right now," Dr. O'Connor said. "You see, the bulk of this machine is in Nevada; the structure is both too heavy and too delicate for transport. And there are other qualifications—"

"I meant theoretically," Burris said.

"Theoretically—" Dr. O'Connor began, and smiled again— "Theoretically, if your mind were being read, this machine would detect it, supposing that the machine were in operating condition and all of the other qualifications had been met. You see, Mr. Burris, no matter how poor a telepath a man may be, he has some slight ability—even if only very slight—to detect the fact that his mind is being read."

"You mean, if somebody was reading my mind, I'd know it?" Burris said. His face showed, Malone realized, that he plainly disbelieved this statement.

"You would know it," Dr. O'Connor said, "but you would never know you knew it. To elucidate: in a normal person—like you, for instance, or even like myself—the state of having one's mind read merely results in a vague, almost sub-conscious feeling of irritation, something that could easily be attributed to minor worries, or fluctuations in one's hormonal balance. The hormonal balance, Mr. Burris, is—"

"Thank you," Burris said with a trace of irritation. "I know what hormones are."

"Ah. Good," Dr. O'Connor said equably. "In any case,

to continue: this machine interprets those specific feelings as indications that the mind is being—ah—'eavesdropped' upon."

You could almost see the quotation marks around what Dr. O'Connor considered slang dropping into place, Malone thought.

"I see," Burris said with a disappointed air. "But what do you mean, it won't detect a telepath? Have you ever actually worked with a telepath?"

"Certainly we have," Dr. O'Connor said. "If we hadn't, how would we be able to tell that the machine was, in fact, indicating the presence of telepathy? The theoretical state of the art is not, at present, sufficiently developed to enable us to—"

"I see," Burris said hurriedly. "Only wait a minute."

"Yes?"

"You mean you've actually got a real mind-reader? You've found one? One that works?"

Dr. O'Connor shook his head sadly. "I'm afraid I should have said, Mr. Burris, that we did once have one," he admitted. "He was, unfortunately, an imbecile, with a mental age between five and six, as nearly as we were ever able to judge."

"An imbecile?" Burris said. "But how were you able to—"

"He could repeat a person's thoughts word for word," Dr. O'Connor said. "Of course, he was utterly incapable of understanding the meaning behind them. That didn't matter; he simply repeated whatever you were thinking. Rather disconcerting."

"I'm sure," Burris said. "But he was really an imbecile? There wasn't any chance of—"

"Of curing him?" Dr. O'Connor said. "None, I'm afraid. We did at one time feel that there had been a mental breakdown early in the boy's life, and, indeed, it's perfectly possible that he was normal for the first year or so. The records we did manage to get on that period, however, were very much confused, and there was never any way of telling anything at all, for certain. It's easy to see what caused the confusion, of course: telepathy in an imbecile is rather an oddity—and any normal adult would probably be rather hesitant about admitting that he was capable of it. That's why we have not found another subject; we must merely sit back and wait for lightning to strike."

Burris sighed. "I see your problem," he said. "But what happened to this imbecile boy of yours?"

"Very sad," Dr. O'Connor said. "Six months ago, at the age of fifteen, the boy simply died. He simply—gave up, and died."

"Gave up?"

"That was as good an explanation as our medical department was able to provide, Mr. Burris. There was some malfunction—but—we like to say that he simply gave up. Living became too difficult for him."

"All right," Burris said after a pause. "This telepath of yours is dead, and there aren't any more where he came from. Or if there are, you don't know how to look for them. All right. But to get back to this machine of yours: it couldn't detect the boy's ability?"

Dr. O'Connor shook his head. "No, I'm afraid not. We've worked hard on that problem at Westinghouse, Mr. Burris, but we haven't yet been able to find a method of actually detecting telepaths."

"But you can detect—"

"That's right," Dr. O'Connor said. "We can detect the fact that a man's mind is being read." He stopped, and his face became suddenly morose. When he spoke again, he sounded guilty, as if he were making an admission that pained him. "Of course, Mr. Burris, there's nothing we can do about a man's mind being read. Nothing whatever." He essayed a grin that didn't look very healthy. "But at least," he said, "you know you're being spied on."

Burris grimaced. There was a little silence while Dr. O'Connor stroked the metal box meditatively, as if it were the head of his beloved.

At last, Burris said: "Dr. O'Connor, how sure can you be of all this?"

The look he received made all the previous conversation seem as warm and friendly as a Christmas party by comparison. It was a look that froze the air of the room into a solid chunk, Malone thought, a chunk you could have chipped pieces from, for souvenirs, later, when Dr. O'Connor had gone and you could get into the room without any danger of being quick-frozen by the man's unfriendly eye.

"Mr. Burris," Dr. O'Connor said in a voice that matched the temperature of his gaze, "please. Remember our slogan."

Malone sighed. He fished in his pocket for a pack of cigarettes, found one, and extracted a single cigarette. He stuck it in his mouth and started fishing in various pockets for his lighter.

He sighed again. Perfectly honestly, he preferred cigars, a habit he'd acquired from the days when he'd filched them from his father's cigar-case. But his mental picture of a fearless and alert young FBI agent didn't include a cigar. Somehow, remembering his father as neither fearless nor, exactly, alert—anyway, not the way the movies and the TV screens liked to picture the words—he had the impression that cigars looked out of place on FBI agents.

And it was, in any case, a small sacrifice to make. He found his lighter and shielded it from the brisk wind. He looked out over water at the Jefferson Memorial, and was surprised that he'd managed to walk as far as he had. Then he stopped thinking about walking, and took a puff of his cigarette, and forced himself to think about the job in hand.

Naturally, the Westinghouse gadget had been declared Ultra Top Secret as soon as it had been worked out. Virtually everything was, these days. And the whole group involved in the machine and its workings had been transferred without delay to the United States Laboratories out in Yucca Flats, Nevada.

Out there in the desert, there just wasn't much to do, Malone supposed, except to play with the machine. And, of course, look at the scenery. But when you've seen one desert, Malone thought confusedly, you've seen them all.

So, the scientists ran experiments on the machine, and

they made a discovery of a kind they hadn't been looking for.

Somebody, they discovered, was picking the brains of the scientists there.

Not the brains of the people working with the telepathy machine.

And not the brains of the people working on the several other Earth-limited projects at Yucca Flats.

They'd been reading the minds of some of the scientists working on the new and highly classified non-rocket space drive.

In other words, the Yucca Flats plant was infested with a telepathic spy. And how do you go about finding a telepath? Malone sighed. Spies that got information in any of the usual ways were tough enough to locate. A telepathic spy was a lot tougher proposition.

Well, one thing about Andrew J. Burris. He had an answer for everything. Malone thought of what his chief had said: "It takes a thief to catch a thief. And if the Westinghouse machine won't locate a telepathic spy, I know what will."

"What?" Malone had asked.

"It's simple," Burris had said. "Another telepath. There has to be one around somewhere. Westinghouse did have one, after all, and the Russians *still* have one. Malone, that's your job: go out and find me a telepath."

Burris had an answer for everything, all right, Malone thought. But he couldn't see where the answer did him very much good. After all, if it takes a telepath to catch a telepath, how do you catch the telepath you're going to use to catch the first telepath?

Malone ran that through his mind again, and then gave it up. It sounded as if it should have made sense, somehow, but it just didn't, and that was all there was to that.

He dropped his cigarette to the ground and mashed it out with the toe of his shoe. Then he looked up.

Out there, over the water, was the Jefferson Memorial. It stood, white in the floodlights, beautiful and untouchable in the darkness. Malone stared at it. What would Thomas Jefferson have done in a crisis like this?

Jefferson, he told himself without much conviction, would have been just as confused as he was.

But he'd have had to find a telepath, Malone thought. Malone determined that he would do likewise, If Thomas Jefferson could do it, the least he, Malone, could do was to give it a good try.

There was only one little problem:

Where, Malone thought, *do I start looking?*

2

Early the next morning, Malone awoke on a plane, heading across the continent toward Nevada. He had gone home to sleep, and he'd had to wake up to get on the plane, and now here he was, waking up again. It seemed, somehow, like a vicious circle.

The engines hummed gently as they pushed the big ship through the middle stratosphere's thinly distributed molecules. Malone looked out at the purple-dark sky and set himself to think out his problem again.

He was still mulling things over when the ship lowered its landing gear and rolled to a stop on the big field near Yucca Flats. Malone sighed and climbed slowly out of his seat. There was a car waiting for him at the airfield, though, and that seemed to presage a smooth time; Malone remembered calling Dr. O'Connor the night before, and congratulated himself on his foresight.

Unfortunately, when he reached the main gate of the high double fence that surrounded the more than ninety square miles of United States Laboratories, he found out that entrance into that sanctum sanctorum of Security wasn't as easy as he'd imagined—not even for an FBI man. His credentials were checked with the kind of minute care Malone had always thought people reserved for disputed art masterpieces, and it was with a great show of reluctance that the Special Security guards passed him inside as far as the office of the Chief Security Officer.

There, the Chief Security Officer himself, a man who could have doubled for Torquemada, eyed Malone with ill-concealed suspicion while he called Burris at FBI headquarters back in Washington.

Burris identified Malone on the video screen and the Chief Security Officer, looking faintly disappointed, stamped the agent's pass and thanked the FBI chief. Malone had the run of the place.

Then he had to find a courier jeep. The Westinghouse division, it seemed, was a good two miles away.

As Malone knew perfectly well, the main portion of the entire Yucca Flats area was devoted solely to research on the new space drive which was expected to make the rocket as obsolete as the blunderbuss—at least as far as space travel was concerned. Not, Malone thought uneasily, that the blunderbuss had ever been used for space travel, but—

He got off the subject hurriedly. The jeep whizzed by buildings, most of them devoted to aspects of the non-rocket drive. The other projects based at Yucca Flats had to share what space was left—and that included, of course, the Westinghouse research project.

It turned out to be a single, rather small white building with a fence around it. The fence bothered Malone a little, but there was no need to worry; this time he was introduced at once into Dr. O'Connor's office. It was panelled in wallpaper manufactured to look like pine, and the telepathy expert sat behind a large black desk bigger than any Malone had ever seen in the FBI offices. There wasn't a scrap of paper on the desk; its surface was smooth and shiny, and behind it the nearly transparent Dr. Thomas O'Connor was close to invisible.

He looked, in person, just about the same as he'd looked on the FBI tapes. Malone closed the door of the office behind him, looked for a chair and didn't find one. In Dr. O'Connor's office, it was perfectly obvious, Dr. O'Connor sat down. You stood, and were uncomfortable.

Malone took off his hat. He reached across the desk to shake hands with the telepathy expert, and Dr. O'Connor gave him a limp fragile paw. "Thanks for giving me a little time," Malone said. "I really appreciate it." He smiled across the desk. His feet were already beginning to hurt.

"Not at all," Dr. O'Connor said, returning the smile with one of his own special quick-frozen brand. "I realize how important FBI work is to all of us, Mr. Malone. What can I do to help you?"

Malone shifted his feet. "I'm afraid I wasn't very specific on the phone last night," he said. "It wasn't anything I wanted to discuss over a line that might have been tapped. You see, I'm on the telepathy case."

Dr. O'Connor's eyes widened the merest trifle. "I see," he said. "Well, I'll certainly do everything I can to help you."

"Fine," Malone said. "Let's get right down to business, then. The first thing I want to ask you about is this detector of yours. I understand it's too big to carry around—but how about making a smaller model?"

"Smaller?" Dr. O'Connor permitted himself a ghostly chuckle. "I'm afraid that isn't possible, Mr. Malone. I would be happy to let you have a small model of the machine if we had one available—more than happy. I would like to see such a machine myself, as a matter of fact. Unfortunately, Mr. Malone—"

"There just isn't one, right?" Malone said.

"Correct," Dr. O'Connor said. "And there are a few

other factors. In the first place, the person being analyzed has to be in a specially shielded room, such as is used in encephalographic analysis. Otherwise, the mental activity of the other persons around him would interfere with the analysis." He frowned a little. "I could wish that we knew a bit more about psionic machines. The trouble with the present device, frankly, is that it is partly psionic and partly electronic, and we can't be entirely sure where one part leaves off and the other begins. Very trying. Very trying indeed."

"I'll bet it is," Malone said sympathetically, wishing he understood what Dr. O'Connor was talking about.

The telepathy expert sighed. "However," he said, "we keep working at it." Then he looked at Malone expectantly.

Malone shrugged. "Well, if I can't carry the thing around, I guess that's that," he said. "But here's the next question: do you happen to know the maximum range of a telepath? I mean: how far away can he get from another person and still read his mind?"

Dr. O'Connor frowned again. "We don't have definite information on that, I'm afraid," he said. "Poor little Charlie was rather difficult to work with. He was mentally incapable of co-operating in any way, you see."

"Little Charlie?"

"Charles O'Neill was the name of the telepath we worked with," Dr. O'Connor explained.

"I remember," Malone said. The name had been on one of the tapes, but he just hadn't associated "Charles O'Neill" with "Little Charlie." He felt as if he'd been caught with his homework undone. "How did you manage to find him, anyway?" he said. Maybe, if he knew how Westinghouse had found their imbecile-telepath, he'd have some kind of clue that would enable him to find one, too. Anyhow, it was worth a try.

"It wasn't difficult in Charlie's case," Dr. O'Connor said. He smiled. "The child babbled all the time, you see."

"You mean he talked about being a telepath?"

Dr. O'Connor shook his head impatiently. "No," he said. "Not at all. I mean that he babbled. Literally. Here: I've got a sample recording in my files." He got up from his chair and went to the tall gray filing cabinet that hid in a far corner of the pine-panelled room. From a drawer he extracted a spool of common audio tape, and returned to his desk.

"I'm sorry we didn't get full video on this," he said, "but we didn't feel it was necessary." He opened a panel in the upper surface of the desk, and slipped the spool in. "If you like, there are other tapes—"

"Maybe later," Malone said.

Dr. O'Connor nodded and pressed the playback switch at the side of the great desk. For a second the room was silent.

Then there was the hiss of empty tape, and a brisk masculine voice that overrode it:

"Westinghouse Laboratories," it said, "sixteen April nineteen-seventy. Dr. Walker speaking. The voice you are about to hear belongs to Charles O'Neill: chronological age fourteen years, three months; mental age, approximately five years. Further data on this case will be found in the file *O'Neill*."

There was a slight pause, filled with more tape hiss. Then the voice began.

". . . push the switch for record . . . in the park last Wednesday . . . and perhaps a different set of . . . poor kid never makes any sense in . . . trees and leaves all sunny with the . . . electronic components of the reducing stage might be . . . not as predictable when others are around but . . . to go with Sally some night in the . . ."

It was a childish, alto voice, gabbling in a monotone. A phrase would be spoken, the voice would hesitate for just an instant, and then another, totally disconnented phrase would come. The enunciation and pronunciation would vary from phrase to phrase, but the tone remained essentially the same, drained of all emotional content.

". . . in receiving psychocerebral impulses there isn't any . . . nonsense and nothing but nonsense all the . . . tomorrow or maybe Saturday with the girl . . . tube might be replaceable only if . . . something ought to be done for the . . . Saturday would be a good time for . . . work on the schematics tonight if . . ."

There was a click as the tape was turned off, and Dr. O'Connor looked up.

"It doesn't make much sense," Malone said. "But the kid sure has a hell of a vocabulary for an imbecile."

"Vocabulary?" Dr. O'Connor said softly.

"That's right," Malone said. "Where'd an imbecile get words like 'psychocerebral?' I don't think I know what that means, myself."

"Ah," Dr. O'Connor said. "But that's not *his* vocabulary, you see. What Charlie is doing is simply repeating the thoughts of those around him. He jumps from mind to mind, simply repeating whatever he receives." His face assumed the expression of a man remembering a bad taste in his mouth. "That's how we found him out, Mr. Malone," he said. "It's rather startling to look at a blithering idiot and have him suddenly repeat the very thought that's in your mind."

Malone nodded unhappily. It didn't seem as if O'Connor's information was going to be a lot of help as far as catching a telepath was concerned. An imbecile, apparently, would give himself away if he were a telepath. But nobody else seemed to be likely to do that. And imbeciles didn't look like very good material for catching spies with.

Then he brightened. "Doctor, is it possible that the spy we're looking for really isn't a spy?"

"Eh?"

"I mean, suppose he's an imbecile, too? I doubt whether an imbecile would really be a spy, if you see what I mean."

Dr. O'Connor appeared to consider the notion. After a little while he said: "It is, I suppose, possible. But the readings on the machine don't give us the same timing as they did in Charlie's case—or even the same sort of timing."

"I don't quite follow you," Malone said. Truthfully, he felt about three miles behind. But perhaps everything would clear up soon. He hoped so. On top of everything else, his feet were now hurting a lot more.

"Perhaps if I describe one of the tests we ran," Dr. O'Connor said, "things will be somewhat clearer." He leaned back in his chair. Malone shifted his feet again and transferred his hat from his right to his left hand.

"We put one of our test subjects in the insulated room," Dr. O'Connor said, "and connected him to the detector. He was to read from a book—a book that was not too common. This was, of course, to obviate the chance that some other person nearby might be reading it, or might have read it in the past. We picked *The Blood is the Death* by Hieronymus Melanchthon, which, as you may know, is a very rare book indeed."

"Sure," Malone said. He had never heard of the book, but he was, after all, willing to take Dr. O'Connor's word for it.

The telepathy expert went on: "Our test subject read it carefully, scanning rather than skimming. Cameras recorded the movements of his eyes in order for us to tell just what he was reading at any given moment, in order to correlate what was going on in his mind with the reactions of the machine's indicators, if you follow me."

Malone nodded helplessly.

"At the same time," Dr. O'Connor continued blithely, "we had Charlie in a nearby room, recording his babblings. Every so often, he would come out with quotations from *The Blood is the Death,* and these quotations corresponded exactly with what our test subject was reading at the time, and also corresponded with the abnormal fluctuations of the detector."

Dr. O'Connor paused. Something, Malone realized, was expected of him. He thought of several responses and chose one. "I see," he said.

"But the important thing here," Dr. O'Connor said, "is the timing. You see, Charlie was incapable of continued concentration. He could not keep his mind focused on another mind for very long, before he hopped to still another. The actual amount of time concentrated on any given mind at any single given period varied from a minimum of one point three seconds to a maximum of two point six. The timing samples, when plotted graphically over a period of several months, formed a skewed bell curve with a mode at two point oh seconds."

"Ah," Malone said, wondering if a skewed ball curve

was the same thing as a belled skew curve, and if not, why not?

"It was, in fact," Dr. O'Connor continued relentlessly, "a sudden variation in those timings which convinced us that there was another telepath somewhere in the vicinity. We were conducting a second set of reading experiments, in precisely the same manner as the first set, and, for the first part of the experiment, our figures were substantially the same. But—" He stopped.

"Yes?" Malone said, shifting his feet and trying to take some weight off his left foot by standing on his right leg. Then he stood on his left leg. It didn't seem to do any good.

"I should explain," Dr. O'Connor said, "that we were conducting this series with a new set of test subjects: some of the scientists here at Yucca Flats. We wanted to see if the intelligence quotients of the subjects affected the time of contact which Charlie was able to maintain. Naturally, we picked the men here with the highest IQ's, the two men we have who are in the top echelon of the creative genius class." He cleared his throat. "I did not include myself, of course, since I wished to remain an impartial observer, as much as possible."

"Of course," Malone said without surprise.

"The other two geniuses," Dr. O'Connor said, "the other two geniuses both happen to be connected with the project known as Project Isle—an operation whose function I neither know, nor care to know, anything at all about."

Malone nodded. Project Isle was the non-rocket spaceship. Classified. Top Secret. Ultra Secret. And, he thought, just about anything else you could think of.

"At first," Dr. O'Connor was saying, "our detector recorded the time periods of—ah—mental invasion as being the same as before. Then, one day, anomalies began to appear. The detector showed that the minds of our subjects were being held for as long as two or three minutes. But the phrases repeated by Charlie during these periods showed that his own contact time remained the same; that is, they fell within the same skewed bell curve as before, and the mode remained constant if nothing but the phrase length were recorded."

"Hmm," Malone said, feeling that he ought to be saying something.

Dr. O'Connor didn't notice him. "At first we thought of errors in the detector machine," he went on. "That worried us not somewhat, since our understanding of the detector is definitely limited at this time. We do feel that it would be possible to replace some of the electronic components with appropriate symbolization like that already used in the purely psionic sections, but we have, as yet, been unable to determine exactly which electronic components must be replaced by what symbolic components."

Malone nodded, silently this time. He had the sudden feeling that Dr. O'Connor's flow of words had broken itself up into a vast sea of alphabet soup, and that he, Malone, was occupied in drowning in it.

"However," Dr. O'Connor said, breaking what was left of Malone's train of thought, "young Charlie died soon thereafter, and we decided to go on checking the machine. It was during this period that we found someone else reading the minds of our test subjects—sometimes for a few seconds, sometimes for several minutes."

"Aha," Malone said. Things were beginning to make sense again. *Someone else.* That, of course, was the spy.

"I found," Dr. O'Connor said, "on interrogating the subjects more closely, that they were, in effect, thinking on two levels. They were reading the book mechanically, noting the words and sense, but simply shuttling the material directly into their memories without actually thinking about it. The actual thinking portions of their minds were concentrating on aspects of Project Isle."

There was a little silence.

"In other words," Malone said, "someone was spying on them for information about Project Isle?"

"Precisely," Dr. O'Connor said with a frosty, teacher-to-student smile. "And whoever it was had a much higher concentration time than Charlie had ever attained. He seems to be able to retain contact as long as he can find useful information flowing in the mind being read."

"Wait a minute," Malone said. "Wait a minute. If this spy is so clever, how come he didn't read *your* mind?"

"It is very likely that he has," O'Connor said. "What does that have to do with it?"

"Well," Malone said, "if he knows you and your group are working on telepathy and can detect what he's doing, why didn't he just hold off on the minds of those geniuses when they were being tested in your machine?"

Dr. O'Connor frowned. "I'm afraid that I can't be sure," he said, and it was clear from his tone that, if Dr. Thomas O'Connor wasn't sure, no one in the entire world was, had been, or ever would be. "I do have a theory, however," he said, brightening up a trifle.

Malone waited patiently.

"He must know our limitations," Dr. O'Connor said at last. "He must be perfectly well aware that there's not a single thing we can *do* about him. He must know that we can neither find nor stop him. Why should he worry? He can afford to ignore us—or even bait us. We're helpless, and he knows it."

That, Malone thought, was about the most cheerless thought he had heard in some time.

"You mentioned that you had an insulated room," the FBI agent said after a while. "Couldn't you let your men think in there?"

Dr. O'Connor sighed. "The room is shielded against magnetic fields and electro-magnetic radiation. It is perfectly transparent to psionic phenomena, just as it is to gravitational fields."

"Oh," Malone said. He realized rapidly that his question had been a little silly to begin with, since the insulated room had been the place where all the tests had been conducted in the first place. "I don't want to take up too much of your time, Doctor," he said after a pause, "but there are a couple of other questions."

"Go right ahead," Dr. O'Connor said. "I'm sure I'll be able to help you."

Malone thought of mentioning how little help the Doctor had been to date, but decided against it. Why antagonize a perfectly good scientist without any reason? Instead, he selected his first question, and asked it. "Have you got any idea how we might lay our hands on another telepath? Preferably one that's not an imbecile, of course."

Dr. O'Connor's expression changed from patient wisdom to irritation. "I wish we could, Mr. Malone. I wish we could. We certainly need one here to help us here with our work—and I'm sure that your work is important, too. But I'm afraid we have no ideas at all about finding another telepath. Finding little Charlie was purely fortuitous—purely, Mr. Malone, fortuitous."

"Ah," Malone said. "Sure. Of course." He thought rapidly and discovered that he couldn't come up with one more question. As a matter of fact, he'd asked a couple of questions already, and he could barely remember the answers. "Well," he said, "I guess that's about it, then, Doctor. If you come across anything else, be sure and let me know."

He leaned across the desk, extending a hand. "And thanks for your time," he added.

Dr. O'Connor stood up and shook his hand. "No trouble, I assure you," he said. "And I'll certainly give you all the information I can."

Malone turned and walked out. Surprisingly, he discovered that his feet and legs still worked. He had thought they'd turned to stone in the office long before.

It was on the plane back to Washington that Malone got his first inkling of an idea.

The only telepath that the Westinghouse boys had been able to turn up was Charles O'Neill, the youthful imbecile.

All right, then. Suppose there were another like him. Imbeciles weren't very difficult to locate. Most of them would be in institutions, and the others would certainly be on record. It might be possible to find someone, anyway, who could be handled and used as a tool to find a telepathic spy.

And—happy thought!—maybe one of them would turn out to be a high-grade imbecile, or even a moron.

Even if they only turned up another imbecile, he thought

wearily, at least Dr. O'Connor would have something to work with.

He reported back to Burris when he arrived in Washington, told him about the interview with Dr. O'Connor, and explained what had come to seem a rather feeble brainstorm.

"It doesn't seem too productive," Burris said, with a shade of disappointment in his voice, "but we'll try it."

At that, it was a better verdict than Malone had tried for. Though, of course, it meant extra work for him.

Orders went out to field agents all over the United States, and, quietly but efficiently, the FBI went to work. Agents began to probe and pry and poke their noses into the files and data sheets of every mental institution in the fifty states—as far, at any rate, as they were able.

And Kenneth J. Malone was in the lead.

There had been some talk of his staying in Washington to collate the reports as they came in, but that had sounded even worse than having to visit hospitals. "You don't need me to do a job like that," he'd told Burris. "Let's face it, Chief: if we find a telepath the agent who finds him will say so. If we don't, he'll say that, too. You could get a chimpanzee to collate reports like that."

Burris looked at him speculatively, and for one horrible second Malone could almost hear him sending out an order to find, and hire, a chimpanzee (after Security clearance, of course, for whatever organizations a chimpanzee could join). But all he said, in what was almost a mild voice, was: "All right, Malone. And don't call me Chief."

The very mildness of his tone showed how worried the man was, Malone realized, and he set out for the first hospital on his own list with grim determination written all over his face and a heartbeat that seemed to hammer at him that his country expected every man to do his duty.

"I find my duty hard to do today," he murmured under his breath. It was all right to tell himself that he had to find a telepath. But how did you go about it? Did you just knock on hospital doors and ask them if they had anybody who could read minds?

"You know," Malone told himself in a surprised tone, "that isn't such a bad idea." It would, at any rate, let him know whether the hospital had any patients who *thought* they could read minds. From them on, it would probably be simple to apply a test, and separate the telepathic sheep from the psychotic goats.

The image that created in his mind was so odd that Malone, in self-defense, stopped thinking altogether until he'd reached the first hospital, a small place situated in the shrinking countryside West of Washington.

It was called, he knew, the Rice Pavilion.

The place was small, and white. It bore a faint resemblance to Monticello, but then that was true, Malone reflected, of eight out of ten public buildings of all sorts. The front door was large and opaque, and Malone went up the winding driveway, climbed a short flight of marble steps, and rapped sharply.

The door opened instantly.

"Yes?" said the man inside, a tall, balding fellow wearing doctor's whites and a sad, bloodhound-like expression.

"Yes," Malone said automatically. "I mean—my name is Kenneth J. Malone."

"Mine," said the bloodhound, "is Blake. Doctor Andrew Blake." There was a brief pause. "Is there anything we can do for you?" the doctor went on.

"Well," Malone said, "I'm looking for people who can read minds."

Blake didn't seem at all surprised. He nodded quietly. "Of course," he said. "I understand perfectly."

"Good," Malone told him. "You see, I thought I'd have a little trouble finding—"

"Oh, no trouble at all, I assure you," Blake went on, just as mournfully as ever. "You've come to the right place, believe me, Mr.—ah—"

"Malone," Malone said. "Kenneth J. Frankly, I didn't think I'd hit the jackpot this early—I mean, you were the first on my list—"

The doctor seemed suddenly to realize that the two

of them were standing out on the portico. "Won't you come inside?" he said, with a friendly gesture. He stepped aside and Malone walked through the doorway.

Just inside it, three men grabbed him.

Malone, surprised by this sudden reception, fought with every ounce of his FBI training. But the three men had his surprise on their side, and three against one was heavy odds for any man, trained or not.

His neck placed firmly between one upper and lower arm, his legs pinioned and his arms flailing wildly, Malone managed to shout: "What the hell is this? What's going on?"

Dr. Blake was watching the entire operation from a standpoint a few feet away. He didn't look as if his expression were ever going to change.

"It's all for your own good, Mr. Malone," he said calmly. "Please believe me."

"My God!" Malone said. He caught somebody's face with one hand and then somebody else grabbed the hand and folded it back with irresistible force. He had one arm free, and he tried to use it—but not for long. "You think I'm nuts!" he shouted, as the three men produced a strait-jacket from somewhere and began to cram him into it. "Wait!" he cried, as the canvas began to cramp him. "You're wrong! You're making a terrible mistake!"

"Of course," Dr. Blake said. "But if you'll just relax we'll soon be able to help you—"

The strait-jacket was on. Malone sagged inside it like a rather large and sweaty butterfly rewrapped in a cocoon. Dimly, he realized that he sounded like every other nut in the world. All of them would be sure to tell the doctor and the attendants that they were making a mistake. All of them would claim they were sane.

There was, of course, a slight difference. But how could Malone manage to prove it? The three men held him up.

"Now, now," Dr. Blake said. "You can walk, Mr. Malone. Suppose you just follow me to your room—"

"My room?" Malone said. "Now, you listen to me, Doctor. If you don't take this stuff off me at once I promise you the President will hear of it. And I don't know how he'll take interference in a vital mission—"

"The President?" Blake asked quietly. "What President, Mr. Malone?"

"The President of the United States, damn it!" Malone shouted.

"Hmm," Blake said.

That was no good, either, Malone realized. Every nut would have some sort of direct pipeline to the President, or God, or somebody high up. Nuts were like that.

But he was an FBI Agent. A special agent on a vital mission.

He said so.

"Now, now, Mr. Malone," Blake told him. "Let's get to your room, shall we, and then we can talk things over."

"I can prove it!" Malone told him. The three men picked him up. "My identification is in my pocket—"

"Really?" Blake said.

They started moving down the long front hall.

"All you have to do is take this thing off so I can get at my pockets—" Malone began.

But even he could see that this new plan wasn't going to work, either.

"Take it off?" Blake said. "Oh, certainly, Mr. Malone. Certainly. Just as soon as we have you comfortably settled."

It was ridiculous, Malone told himself as the men carried him away. It couldn't happen: an FBI agent mistaken for a nut, wrapped in a strait-jacket and carried to a padded cell.

Unfortunately, ridiculous or not, it was happening.

And there was absolutely nothing to do about it.

Malone thought with real longing of his nice, safe desk in Washington. Suddenly he discovered in himself a great desire to sit around and collate reports. But no—he had to be a hero. He had to go and get himself involved.

This, he thought, will teach me a great lesson. The next time I get offered a job a chimpanzee can do, I'll start eating bananas.

It was at this point in his reflections that he reached a small door. Dr. Blake opened it and the three men carried Malone inside. He was dumped carefully on the floor. Then the door clanged shut.

Alone, Malone told himself bitterly, at last.

After a minute or so had gone by he began to think about getting out. He could, it occurred to him, scream for help. But that would only bring more attendants, and very possibly Dr. Blake again, and somehow Malone felt that further conversation with Dr. Blake was not likely to lead to any very rational end.

Sooner or later, he knew, they would have to let him loose.

After all, he was an FBI agent, wasn't he?

Alone, in a single cheerless cell, caught up in the toils of a strait-jacket, he began to doubt the fact. Maybe Blake was right; maybe they were all right. Maybe he, Kenneth J. Malone, was totally mad.

He told himself firmly that the idea was ridiculous.

But, then, what wasn't?

The minutes ticked slowly by. After a while the three guards came back, opening the door and filing into the room carefully. Malone, feeling more than ever like something in a cocoon, watched them with interest. They shut the door carefully behind them and stood before him.

"Now, then," one of them said. "We're going to take the jacket off, if you promise to be a good boy."

"Sure," Malone said. "And when you take my clothing, look in the pockets."

"The pockets?"

"To find my FBI identification," Malone said wearily. He only half-believed the idea himself, but half a belief, he told himself confusedly, was better than no mind at all. The attendants nodded solemnly.

"Sure we will," one of them said, "if you're a good boy and don't act up rough on us now. Okay?"

Malone nodded. Carefully, two of the attendants began to unbuckle him while the third stood by for reinforcements. Malone made no fuss.

In five minutes he was naked as—he told himself

—a jay-bird. What was so completely nude about those particular birds escaped him for the moment, but it wasn't important. The three men were all holding various parts of the strait-jacket or of his clothing.

They were still watching him warily.

"Look in the pockets," Malone said.

"Sure," one said. The man holding the jacket reached into it and dropped it as if it were hot.

"Hey," he announced in a sick voice, "the guy's carrying a gun."

"A gun?" the second one asked.

The first one gestured toward the crumpled jacket on the floor. "Look for yourself," he said. "A real honest-to-God gun. I could feel it."

Malone leaned against one wall, looking as nonchalant as it was possible for him to look in the nude. The room being cool, he felt he was succeeding reasonably well. "Try the other pocket," he suggested.

The first attendant gave him a long stare. "What've you got in there, buddy?" he asked. "A howitzer?"

"Jesus," the second attendant said, without moving toward the jacket. "An armed nut. What a world."

"Try the pocket," Malone said.

A second went by. The first attendant bent down slowly, picked up the jacket and slipped his hand into the other inside pocket. He came out with a wallet and flipped it open.

The others looked over his shoulder. There was a long minute of silence.

"Jesus," the second attendant said, as if it were the only word left in the language.

Malone sighed. "There, now," he said. "You see? Suppose you give me back my clothes and let's get down to brass tacks."

It wasn't that simple, of course.

First the attendants had to go and get Dr. Blake, and everybody had to explain everything three or four times, until Malone was just as sick of being an FBI agent as he had ever been of being a padded-cell case. But, at last, he stood before Dr. Blake in the corridor outside, once again fully dressed. Slightly rumpled, of course, but fully dressed. It did, Malone thought, make a difference, and if clothes didn't exactly make the man they were a long way from a hindrance.

"Mr. Malone," Blake was saying, "I want to offer my apologies—"

"Perfectly okay," Malone said agreeably. "But I would like to know something. Do you treat all your visitors like this? I mean—the milkman, the mailman, relatives of patients—"

"It's not often we get someone here who claims to be from the FBI," Blake said. "And naturally our first thought was that—well, sometimes a patient will come in, just give himself up, so to speak. His unconscious mind knows that he needs help, and so he comes to us. We try to help him."

Privately, Malone told himself that it was a hell of a way to run a hospital. Aloud, all he said was: "Sure. I undersand perfectly, Doctor."

Dr. Blake nodded. "And now," he said, "what did you want to talk to me about?"

"Just a minute." Malone closed his eyes. He'd told Burris he would check in, and he was late. "Have you got a phone I can use?"

"Certainly," Blake said, and led him down the corridor to a small office. Malone went to the phone at one end and began dialing even before Blake shut the door and left him alone.

The screen lit up instantly with Burris' face. "Malone, where the hell have you been?" the head of the FBI roared. "I've been trying to get in touch with you—"

"Sorry," Malone said. "I was tied up."

"What do you mean, tied up?" Burris said. "Do you know I was just about to send out a general search order? I thought they'd got you."

"They?" Malone said, interested. "Who?"

"How the hell would I know who?" Burris roared.

"Well, nobody got me," Malone said. "I've been investigating Rice Pavillion, just like I'm supposed to do."

"Then why didn't you check in?" Burris asked.

Malone sighed. "Because I got myself locked up," he said, and explained. Burris listened with patience.

When Malone was finished, Burris said: "You're coming right on back."

"But—"

"No arguments," Burris told him. "If you're going to let things like that happen to you you're better off here. Besides, there are plenty of men doing the actual searching. There's no need—"

Secretly, Malone felt relief. "Well, all right," he said. "But let me check out this place first, will you?"

"Go ahead," Burris said. "But get right on back here."

Malone agreed and snapped the phone off. Then he turned back to find Dr. Blake.

Examining hospital records was not an easy job. The inalienable right of a physician to refuse to disclose confidences respecting a patient applied even to idiots, imbecile and morons. But Malone had a slight edge, due to Dr. Blake's embarrassment, and he put it mercilessly to work.

For all the good it did him he might as well have stayed in his cell. There wasn't even the slightest suspicion in any record that any of the Rice Pavilion patients were telepathic.

"Are you sure that's what you're looking for?" Blake asked him, some hours later.

"I'm sure," Malone said. "When you eliminate the impossible, whatever remains, however improbable, must be the truth."

"Oh," Blake said. After a second he added: "What does that mean?"

Malone shrugged. "It's an old saying," he told the doctor. "It doesn't have to mean anything. It just sounds good."

"Oh," Blake said again.

After a while, Malone said farewell to good old Rice Pavilion, and headed back to Washington. There, he told himself, everything would be peaceful.

And so it was. Peaceful and dispiriting.

Every agent had problems getting reports from hospitals—and not even the FBI could open the private files of a licensed and registered psychiatrist.

But the field agents did the best they could and, considering the circumstances, their best was pretty good.

Malone, meanwhile, put in two weeks sitting glumly at his Washington desk and checking reports as they arrived. They were uniformly depressing. The United States of America contained more sub-normal minds than Malone cared to think about. There seemed to be enough of them to explain the results of any election you were unhappy over. Unfortunately, sub-normal was all you could call them. Like the patients at Rice Pavilion, not one of them appeared to possess any abnormal psionic abilities whatever.

There were a couple who were reputed to be poltergeists—but in neither case was there a single shred of evidence to substantiate the claim.

At the end of the second week, Malone was just about convinced that his idea had been a total washout. He himself had been locked up in a padded cell, and other agents had spent a full fortnight digging up imbeciles, while the spy at Yucca Flats had been going right on his merry way, scooping information out of the men at Project Isle as though he were scooping beans out of a pot. And, very likely, laughing himself silly at the feeble efforts of the FBI.

Who could he be?

Anyone, Malone told himself unhappily. Anyone at all. He could be the janitor who swept out the buildings, one of the guards at the gate, one of the minor technicians on another project, or even some old prospector wandering around the desert with a scintillation counter.

Is there any limit to telepathic range?

The spy could even be sitting quietly in an armchair in the Kremlin, probing through several thousand miles of solid earth to peep into the brains of the men on Project Isle.

That was, to say the very least, a depressing idea.

Malone found he had to assume that the spy was in the United States—that, in other words, there was some effective range to telepathic communication. Otherwise, there was no point in bothering to continue the search.

Therefore, he found one other thing to do. He alerted every agent to the job of discovering how the spy was getting his information out of the country.

He doubted that it would turn up anything, but it was a chance. And Malone hoped desperately for it, because he was beginning to be sure that the field agents were never going to turn up any telepathic imbeciles.

He was right.
They never did.

3

The telephone rang.

Malone rolled over on the couch and muttered four words under his breath. Was it absolutely necessary for someone to call him at seven in the morning?

He grabbed at the receiver with one hand, and picked up his cigar from the ashtray with the other. It was bad enough to be awakened from a sound sleep—but when a man hadn't been sleeping at all, it was even worse.

He'd been sitting up since before five that morning, worrying about the telepathic spy, and at the moment he wanted sleep more than he wanted phone calls.

"Gur?" he said, sleepily and angrily, thankful that he'd never had a visiphone installed in his apartment. A taste for blondes was apparently hereditary. At any rate, Malone felt he had inherited it from his father, and he didn't want any visible strangers calling him at odd hours to interfere with his process of collection and research.

He blinked at the audio circuit, and a feminine voice said: "Mr. Kenneth J. Malone?"

"Who's this?" Malone said peevishly, beginning to discover himself capable of semirational English speech.

"Long distance from San Francisco," the voice said.

"It certainly is," Malone said. "Who's calling?"

"San Francisco is calling," the voice said primly.

Malone repressed a desire to tell the voice that he didn't want to talk to St. Francis, not even in Spanish, and said instead: "*Who* in San Francisco?"

There was a momentary hiatus, and then the voice said: "Mr. Thomas Boyd is calling, sir. He says this is a scramble call."

Malone took a drag from his cigar and closed his eyes. Obviously the call was a scramble. If it had been clear, the man would have dialled direct, instead of going through what Malone now recognized as an operator.

"Mr. Boyd says he is the Agent-in-Charge of the San Francisco office of the FBI," the voice offered.

"And quite right, too," Malone told her. "All right. Put him on."

"One moment," There was a pause, a click, another pause and then another click. At last the operator said: "Your party is ready, sir."

Then there was still another pause. Malone stared at the audio receiver. He began to whistle *When Irish Eyes Are Smiling*.

. . . And the sound of Irish laughter . . .

"Hello? Malone?"

"I'm here, Tom," Malone said guiltily. "This is me. What's the trouble?"

"Trouble?" Boyd said. "There isn't any trouble. Well, not really. Or maybe it is. I don't know."

Malone scowled at the audio receiver, and for the first time wished he had gone ahead and had a video circuit put in, so that Boyd could see the horrendous expression on his face.

"Look," he said. "It's seven here and that's too early. Out there, it's four, and that's practically ridiculous. What's so important?"

He knew perfectly well that Boyd wasn't calling him just for the fun of it. The man was a damned good agent. But why a call at this hour?

Malone muttered under his breath. Then, self-consciously, he squashed out his cigar and lit a cigarette while Boyd was saying: "Ken, I think we may have found what you've been looking for."

It wasn't safe to say too much, even over a scrambled circuit. But Malone got the message without difficulty.

"Yeah?" he said, sitting up on the edge of the couch. "You sure?"

"Well," Boyd said, "no. Not absolutely sure. Not absolutely. But it is worth your taking a personal look, I think."

"Ah," Malone said cautiously. "An imbecile?"

"No," Boyd said flatly. "Not an imbecile. Definitely not an imbecile. As a matter of fact, a hell of a fat long way from an imbecile."

Malone glanced at his watch and skimmed over the airline timetables in his mind. "I'll be there nine o'clock, your time," he said. "Have a car waiting for me at the field."

As usual, Malone managed to sleep better on the plane than he'd been able to do at home. He slept so well, in fact, that he was still groggy when he stepped into the waiting car.

"Good to see you, Ken," Boyd said briskly, as he shook Malone's hand.

"You, too, Tom," Malone said sleepily. "Now what's all this about?" He looked around apprehensively. "No bugs in this car, I hope?" he said.

Boyd gunned the motor and headed toward the San Francisco Freeway. "Better not be," he said, "or I'll fire me a technician or two."

"Well, then," Malone said, relaxing against the upholstery, "where is this guy, and who is he? And how did you find him?"

Boyd looked uncomfortable. It was, somehow, both an awe-inspiring and a slightly risible sight. Six feet one and one-half inches tall in his flat feet, Boyd posted around over two hundred and twenty pounds of bone, flesh and muscle. He swung a pot-belly of startling proportions under the silk shirting he wore, and his face, with its wide nose, small eyes and high forehead, was half highly mature, half startlingly childlike. In an apparent effort to erase those childlike qualities, Boyd sported a fringe of beard and a moustache which reminded Malone of somebody he couldn't quite place.

But whoever the somebody was, his hair hadn't been black, as Boyd's was. . . .

He decided it didn't make any difference. Anyhow, Boyd was speaking.

"In the first place," he said, "it isn't a guy. In the second, I'm not exactly sure who it is. And in the third, Ken, I didn't find it."

There was a little silence.

"Don't tell me," Malone said. "It's a telepathic horse, isn't it? Tom, I just don't think I could stand a telepathic horse. . . ."

"No," Boyd said hastily. "No. Not at all. No horse. It's a dame. I mean a lady." He looked away from the road and flashed a glance at Malone. His eyes seemed to be pleading for something—understanding, possibly, Malone thought. "Frankly," Boyd said, "I'd rather not tell you anything about her just yet. I'd rather you met her first. Then you could make up your own mind. All right?"

"All right," Malone said wearily. "Do it your own way. How far do we have to go?"

"Just about an hour's drive," Boyd said. "That's all."

Malone slumped back in the seat and pushed his hat over his eyes. "Fine," he said. "Suppose you wake me up when we get there."

But, groggy as he was, he couldn't sleep. He wished

he'd had some coffee on the plane. Maybe it would have made him feel better.

Then again, coffee was only coffee. True, he had never acquired his father's taste for gin (and imagined, therefore, that it wasn't hereditary, like a taste for blondes), but there was always bourbon.

He thought about bourbon for a few minutes. It was a nice thought. It warmed him and made him feel a lot better. After a while, he even felt awake enough to do some talking.

He pushed his hat back and struggled to a reasonable sitting position. "I don't suppose you have a drink hidden away in the car somewhere?" he said tentatively. "Or would the technicians have found that, too?"

"Better not have," Boyd said in the same tone as before, "or I'll fire a couple of technicians." He grinned without turning. "It's in the door compartment, next to the forty-five cartridges and the Tommy-gun."

Malone opened the compartment in the thick door of the car and extracted a bottle. It was Christian Brothers Brandy instead of the bourbon he had been thinking about, but he discovered that he didn't mind at all. It went down as smoothly as milk.

Boyd glanced at it momentarily as Malone screwed the top back on.

"No," Malone said in answer to the unspoken question. "You're driving." Then he settled back again and tipped his hat forward.

He didn't sleep a wink. He was perfectly sure of that. But it wasn't over two seconds later that Boyd said: "We're here, Ken. Wake up."

"Whadyamean, wakep," Malone said. "I wasn't asleep." He thumbed his hat back and sat up rapidly. "Where's 'here?' "

"Bayview Neuropsychiatric Hospital," Boyd said. "This is where Dr. Harman works, you know."

"No," Malone said. "As a matter of fact, I don't know. You didn't tell me—remember? And who is Dr. Harman, anyhow?"

The car was moving up a long, curving driveway

toward a large, lawn-surrounded building. Boyd spoke without looking away from the road.

"Well," he said, "this Dr. Wilson Harman is the man who phoned us yesterday. One of my field agents was out here asking around about imbeciles and so on. Found nothing, by the way. And then this Dr. Harman called, later. Said he had someone here I might be interested in. So I came on out myself for a look, yesterday afternoon—after all, we had instructions to follow up every possible lead."

"I know," Malone said. "I wrote them."

"Oh," Boyd said. "Sure. Well, anyhow, I talked to this dame. Lady."

"And?"

"And I talked to her," Boyd said. "I'm not entirely sure of anything myself. But—well, hell. You take a look at her."

He pulled the car up to a parking space, slid nonchalantly into a slot marked *Reserved—Executive Director Sutton,* and slid out from under the wheel while Malone got out the other side.

They marched up the broad steps, through the doorway and into the glass-fronted office of the receptionist.

Boyd showed her his little golden badge, and got an appropriate gasp. "FBI," he said. "Dr. Harman's expecting us."

The wait wasn't over fifteen seconds. Boyd and Malone marched down the hall and around a couple of corners, and came to the doctor's office. The door was opaqued glass with nothing but a room number stencilled on it. Without ceremony, Boyd pushed the door open. Malone followed him inside.

The office was small but sunny. Dr. Wilson Harman sat behind a blond-wood desk, a little man with crew-cut blond hair and rimless eyeglasses, who looked about thirty-two and couldn't possibly, Malone thought, have been anywhere near that young. On a second look, Malone noticed a better age indication in the eyes and forehead, and revised his first guess upward between ten and fifteen years.

"Come in, gentlemen," Dr. Harman called. His voice was that rarity, a really loud high tenor.

"Dr. Harman," Boyd said, "this is my superior, Mr. Malone. We'd like to have a talk with Miss Thompson, if we might."

"I anticipated that, sir," Dr. Harman said. "Miss Thompson is in the next room. Have you explained to Mr. Malone that—"

"I haven't explained a thing," Boyd said quickly, and added in what was obviously intended to be a casual tone: "Mr. Malone wants to get a picture of Miss Thompson directly—without any preconceptions."

"I see," Dr. Harman said. "Very well, gentlemen. Through this door."

He opened the door in the right-hand wall of the room, and Malone took one look. It was a long, long look. Standing framed in the doorway, dressed in the starched white of a nurse's uniform, was the most beautiful blonde he had ever seen.

She had curves. She definitely had curves. As a matter of fact, Malone didn't really think he had ever seen curves before. These were something new and different and truly three-dimensional. But it wasn't the curves, or the long straight lines of her legs, or the quiet beauty of her face, that made her so special. After all, Malone had seen legs and bodies and faces before.

At least, he thought he had. Offhand, he couldn't remember where. Looking at the girl, Malone was ready to write brand-new definitions for every anatomical term. Even a term like "hands." Malone had never seen anything especially arousing in the human hand before —anyway, not when the hand was just lying around, so to speak, attached to its wrist but not doing anything in particular. But these hands, long, slender and tapering, white and cool-looking . . .

And yet, it wasn't just the sheer physical beauty of the girl. She had something else, something more and something different. (*Something borrowed*, Malone thought in a semidelirious haze, *and something blue*.) Personality? Character? Soul?

Whatever it was, Malone decided, this girl had it. She

had enough of it to supply the entire human race, and any others that might exist in the Universe. Malone smiled at the girl and she smiled back.

After seeing the smile, Malone wasn't sure he could still walk evenly. Somehow, though, he managed to go over to her and extend his hand. The notion that a telepath would turn out to be this mind-searing Epitome had never crossed his mind, but now, somehow, it seemed perfectly fitting and proper.

"Good morning, Miss Thompson," he said in what he hoped was a winning voice.

The smile disappeared. It was like the sun going out.

The vision appeared to be troubled. Malone was about to volunteer his help—if necessary, for the next seventy years—when she spoke.

"I'm not Miss Thompson," she said.

"This is one of our nurses," Dr. Harman put in. "Miss Wilson, Mr. Malone. And Mr. Boyd. Miss Thompson, gentlemen, is over there."

Malone turned.

There, in a corner of the room, an old lady sat. She was a small old lady, with apple-red cheeks and twinkling eyes. She held some knitting in her hands, and she smiled up at the FBI men as if they were her grandsons come for tea and cookies, of a Sunday afternoon.

She had snow-white hair that shone like a crown around her old head in the lights of the room. Malone blinked at her. She didn't disappear.

"You're Miss Thompson?" he said.

She smiled sweetly. "Oh, my, no," she said.

There was a long silence. Malone looked at her. Then he looked at the unbelievably beautiful Miss Wilson. Then he looked at Dr. Harman. And, at last, he looked at Boyd.

"All right," he said. "I get it. *You're* Miss Thompson."

"Now, wait a minute, Malone," Boyd began.

"Wait a minute?" Malone said. "There are four people here, not counting me. I know I'm not Miss Thompson. I never was, not even as a child. And Dr. Harman isn't, and Miss Wilson isn't, and Whistler's Great-Grandmother isn't, either. So you must be. Unless she isn't here. Or unless she's invisible. Or unless I'm crazy."

"It isn't *you*, Malone," Boyd said.

"What isn't me?"

"That's crazy," Boyd said.

"Okay," Malone said. "I'm not crazy. Then will somebody please tell me——"

The little old lady cleared her throat. A silence fell. When it was complete she spoke, and her voice was as sweet and kindly as anything Malone had ever heard.

"You may call me Miss Thompson," she said. "For the present, at any rate. They all do here. It's a pseudonym I have to use."

"A pseudonym?" Malone said.

"You see, Mr. Malone," Miss Wilson began.

Malone stopped her. "Don't talk," he said. "I have to concentrate and if you talk I can barely think." He took off his hat suddenly, and began twisting the brim in his hands. "You understand, don't you?"

The trace of a smile appeared on her face. "I think I do," she said.

"Now," Malone said. "You're Miss Thompson, but not really, because you have to use a pseudonym." He blinked at the little old lady. "Why?"

"Well," she said, "otherwise people would find out about my little secret."

"Your little secret," Malone said.

"That's right," the little old lady said. "I'm immortal, you see."

Malone said: "Oh." Then he kept quiet for a long time. It didn't seem to him that anyone in the room was breathing.

He said: "Oh," again, but it didn't sound any better than it had the first time. He tried another phrase. "You're immortal," he said.

"That's right," the little old lady agreed sweetly.

There was only one other question to ask, and Malone set his teeth grimly and asked it. It came out just a trifle indistinct, but the little old lady nodded.

"My real name?" she said. "Elizabeth. Elizabeth Tudor, of course. I used to be Queen."

"Of England," Malone said faintly.

"Malone, look—" Boyd began.

"Let me get it all at once," Malone told him. "I'm strong. I can take it." He twisted his hat again and turned back to the little old lady.

"You're immortal, and you're not really Miss Thompson, but Queen Elizabeth I?" he said slowly.

"That's right," she said. "How clever of you. Of course, after little Jimmy—cousin Mary's boy, I mean—said I was dead and claimed the Throne, I decided to change my name and all. And that's what I did. But I am Elizabeth Regina." She smiled, and her eyes twinkled merrily. Malone stared at her for a long minute.

Burris, he thought, *is going to love this.*

"Oh, I'm so glad," the little old lady said. "Do you really think he will? Because I'm sure I'll like your Mr. Burris, too. All of you FBI men are so charming. Just like poor, poor Essex."

Well, Malone told himself, that was that. He'd found himself a telepath.

And she wasn't an imbecile.

Oh, no. That would have been simple.

Instead, she was battier than a cathedral spire.

The long silence was broken by the voice of Miss Wilson.

"Mr. Malone," she said. "You've been thinking." She stopped. "I mean, you've been so quiet."

"I like being quiet," Malone said patiently. "Besides—" He stopped and turned to the little old lady. *Can you really read my mind?* he thought deliberately. After a second he added: *... your Majesty?*

"How sweet of you, Mr. Malone," she said. "Nobody's called me that for centuries. But of course I can. Although it's not reading, really. After all, that would be like asking if I can read your voice. Of course I can, Mr. Malone."

"That does it," Malone said. "I'm not a hard man to convince. And when I see the truth, I'm the first one to admit it, even if it makes me look like a nut." He turned back to the little old lady. "Begging your pardon," he said.

"Oh, my," the little old lady said. "I really don't mind at all. Sticks and stones, you know, can break my bones. But being called nuts, Mr. Malone, can never hurt me. After all, it's been so many years—so many hundreds of years—"

"Sure," Malone said easily.

Boyd broke in. "Listen, Malone," he said. "Do you mind telling me what the hell is going on?"

"It's very simple," Malone said. "Miss Thompson here—pardon me; I mean Queen Elizabeth I—really is a telepath. That's all. I think I want to lie down somewhere until it goes away."

"Until what goes away?" Miss Wilson said.

Malone stared at her almost without seeing her, if not quite. "Everything," he said. He closed his eyes.

"My goodness," the little old lady said after a second. "Everything's so confused. Poor Mr. Malone is terribly shaken up by everything." She stood up, still holding her knitting, and went across the room. Before the astonished eyes of the doctor and nurse, and Tom Boyd, she patted the FBI agent on the shoulder. "There, there, Mr. Malone," she said. "It will all be perfectly all right. You'll see." Then she returned to her seat.

Malone opened his eyes. "My God," he said. He closed them again but they flew open as if of their own accord. He turned to Dr. Harman. "You called up Boyd here," he said, "and told him that—er—Miss Thompson was a telepath. How'd you know?"

"It's all right," the little old lady put in from her chair. "I don't mind your calling me Miss Thompson, not right now, anyhow."

"Thanks," Malone said faintly.

Dr. Harman was blinking in a kind of befuddled astonishment. "You mean she really *is* a—" He stopped and brought his tenor voice to a squeaking halt, regained his professional poise, and began again. "I'd rather not discuss the patient in her presence, Mr. Malone," he said. "If you'll just come into my office—"

"Oh, *bosh*, Dr. Harman," the little old lady said primly.

57

"I do wish you'd give your own Queen credit for some ability. Goodness knows you think *you're* smart enough."

"Now, now, Miss Thompson," he said in what was obviously his best Grade A Choice Government Inspected couchside manner. "Don't—"

"—upset yourself," she finished for him. "Now, really, Doctor. I know what you're going to tell them."

"But Miss Thompson, I—"

"You didn't honestly think I *was* a telepath," the little old lady said. "Heavens, we know that. And you're going to tell them how I used to say I could read minds—oh, years and years ago. And because of that you thought it might be worthwhile to tell the FBI about me—which wasn't very kind of you, Doctor, before you know anything about why they wanted somebody like me."

"Now, now, Miss Thompson," Miss Wilson said, walking across the room to put an arm around the little old lady's shoulder. Malone wished for one brief second that he were the little old lady. Maybe if he were a patient in the hospital he would get the same treatment.

He wondered if he could possibly work such a deal.

Then he wondered if it would be worthwhile, being nuts. But of course it would. He was nuts anyhow, wasn't he?

Sure, he told himself. They were all nuts.

"Nobody's going to hurt you," Miss Wilson said. She was talking to the old lady. "You'll be perfectly all right and you don't have to worry about a thing."

"Oh, yes, dear, I know that," the little old lady said. "You only want to help me, dear. You're so kind. And these FBI men really don't mean any harm. But Doctor Harman didn't know that. He just thinks I'm crazy and that's all."

"Please, Miss Thompson—" Dr. Harman began.

"Just crazy, that's all," the little old lady said. She turned away for a second and nobody said anything. Then she turned back. "Do you all know what he's thinking now?" she said. Dr. Harman turned a dull purple, but she ignored him. "He's wondering why I didn't take the trouble to prove all this to you years ago. And besides that, he's thinking about—"

"Miss Thompson," Dr. Harman said. His bedside manner had cracked through and his voice was harsh and strained. "Please."

"Oh, all right," she said, a little petulantly. "If you want to keep all that private."

Malone broke in suddenly, fascinated. "Why didn't you prove you were telepathic before now?" he said.

The little old lady smiled at him. "Why, because you wouldn't have believed me," she said. She dropped her knitting neatly in her lap and folded her hands over it. "None of you *wanted* to believe me," she said, and sniffed. Miss Wilson moved nervously and she looked up. "And don't tell me it's going to be all right. I know it's going to be all right. I'm going to make sure of that."

Malone felt a sudden chill. But it was obvious, he told himself, that the little old lady didn't mean what she was saying. She smiled at him again, and her smile was as sweet and guileless as the smile on the face of his very own sainted grandmother.

Not that Malone remembered his grandmother; she had died before he'd been born. But if he'd had a grandmother, and if he'd remembered her, he was sure she would have had the same sweet smile.

So she couldn't have meant what she'd said. Would Malone's own grandmother make things difficult for him? The very idea was ridiculous.

Dr. Harman opened his mouth, apparently changed his mind, and shut it again. The little old lady turned to him.

"Were you going to ask why I bothered to prove anything to Mr. Malone?" she said. "Of course you were, and I shall tell you. It's because Mr. Malone wanted to believe me. He wants me. He needs me. I'm a telepath, and that's enough for Mr. Malone. Isn't it?"

"Gur," Malone said, taken by surprise. After a second he added: "I guess so."

"You see, Doctor?" the little old lady said.

"But you—" Dr. Harman began.

"I read minds," the little old lady said. "That's right, Doctor. That's what makes me a telepath."

Malone's brain was whirling rapidly, like a distant

galaxy. Telepath was a nice word, he thought. How do you telepath from a road?

Simple.

The road is paved.

Malone thought that was pretty funny, but he didn't laugh. He thought he would never laugh again. He wanted to cry, a little, but he didn't think he'd be able to manage that either.

He twisted his hat, but it didn't make him feel any better. Gradually, he became aware that the little old lady was talking to Dr. Harman again.

"But," she said, "since it will make you feel so much better, Doctor, we give you our Royal permission to retire, and to speak to Mr. Malone alone."

"Malone alone," Dr. Harman muttered. "Hmm. My. Well." He turned and seemed to be surprised that Malone was actually standing near him. "Yes," he said. "Well. Mr. Alone—Mr. Malone—please, whoever you are, just come into my office, please?"

Malone looked at the little old lady. One of her eyes closed and opened. It was an unmistakable wink.

Malone grinned at her in what he hoped was a cheerful manner. "All right," he said to the psychiatrist, "let's go." He turned with the barest trace of regret, and Boyd followed him. Leaving the little old lady and, unfortunately, the startling Miss Wilson, behind, the procession filed back into Dr. Harman's office.

The doctor closed the door, and leaned against it for a second. He looked as though someone had suddenly revealed to him that the world was square. But when he spoke his voice was almost even.

"Sit down, gentlemen," he said, and indicated chairs. "I really—well, I don't know what to say. All this time, all these years, she's been reading my mind! My mind. She's been reading . . . looking right into my mind, or whatever it is.".

"Whatever what is?" Malone asked, sincerely interested. He had dropped gratefully into a chair near Boyd's, across the desk from Dr. Harman.

"Whatever my *mind* is," Dr. Harmon said. "Reading it. Oh, my."

"Dr. Harman," Malone began, but the psychiatrist gave him a bright blank stare.

"Don't you understand" he said. "She's a telepath."

"We—"

The phone on Dr. Harman's desk chimed gently. He glanced at it and said: "Excuse me. The phone." He picked up the receiver and said: "Hello?"

There was no image on the screen.

But the voice was image enough. "This is Andrew J. Burris," it said. "Is Kenneth J. Malone there?"

"Mr. Malone?" the psychiatrist said. "I mean, Mr. Burris? Mr. Malone is here. Yes. Oh, my. Do you want to talk to him?"

"No, you idiot," the voice said. "I just want to know if he's all tucked in."

"Tucked in?" Dr. Harman gave the phone a sudden smile. "A joke," he said. "It is a joke, isn't it? The way things have been happening, you never know whether—"

"A joke," Burris' voice said. "That's right. Yes. Am I talking to one of the patients?"

Dr. Harman gulped, got mad, and thought better of it. At last he said, very gently; "I'm not at all sure," and handed the phone to Malone.

The FBI agent said: "Hello, Chief. Things are a little confused."

Burris' face appeared on the screen. "Confused, sure," he said. "I feel confused already." He took a breath. "I called the San Francisco office, and they told me you and Boyd were out there. What's going on?"

Malone said cautiously: "We've found a telepath."

Burris' eyes widened slightly. "Another one?"

"What are you talking about, another one?" Malone said. "We have one. Does anybody else have any more?"

"Well," Burris said, "we just got a report on another one—maybe. Besides yours, I mean."

"I hope the one you've got is in better shape than the one I've got," Malone said. He took a deep breath, and then spat it all out at once: "The one we've found is a little old lady. She thinks she's Queen Elizabeth I. She's a telepath, sure, but she's nuts."

"Queen Elizabeth?" Burris said. "Of England?"

"That's right," Malone said. He held his breath.

"Damn it," Burris exploded, "they've already got one!"

Malone sighed. "This is another one," he said. "Or, rather, the original one. She also claims she's immortal."

"Lives forever?" Burris said. "You mean like that?"

"Immortal," Malone said. "Right."

Burris nodded. Then he looked worried. "Tell me, Malone," he said. "She *isn't*, is she?"

"Isn't immortal, you mean?" Malone said. Burris nodded. Malone said confidently: "Of course not."

There was a little pause. Malone thought things over. Hell, maybe she was immortal. Stranger things had happened, hadn't they?

He looked over at Dr. Harman. "How about that?" he said. "Could she be immortal?"

The psychiatrist shook his head decisively. "She's been here for over forty years, Mr. Malone, ever since her late teens. Her records show all that, and her birth certificate is in perfect order. Not a chance."

Malone sighed and turned back to the phone. "Of course she isn't immortal, Chief," he said. "She couldn't be. Nobody is. Just a nut."

"I was afraid of that," Burris said.

"Afraid?" Malone said.

Burris nodded. "We've got another one, or anyhow we think we have," he said. "If he checks out, that is. Right here in Washington."

"Not at—Rice Pavilion?" Malone asked.

"No," Burris said absently. "St. Elizabeths."

Malone sighed. "Another nut?"

"Strait-jacket case," Burris said. "Delusions of persecution, they tell me, and paranoia, and a whole lot of other things that sound nasty as hell. I can't pronounce any of them, and that's always a bad sign."

"Can he talk?" Malone said.

"Who knows?" Burris told him, and shrugged. "I'm sending him on out to Yucca Flats anyhow, under guard. You might find a use for him."

"Oh, sure," Malone said. "We can use him as a horrible example. Suppose he can't talk, or do anything? Suppose he turns violent? Suppose—"

"We can't afford to overlook a thing," Burris said, looking stern.

Once again, Malone sighed deeply. "I know," he said. "But all the same—"

"Don't worry about a thing, Malone," Burris said with a palpably false air of confidence. "Everything is going to be perfectly all right." He looked like a man trying very hard to sell the Brooklyn Bridge to a born New Yorker. "You get this Queen Elizabeth of yours out of there and take her to Yucca Flats, too," he added.

Malone considered the possibilities that were opening up. Maybe, after all, they were going to find more telepaths. And maybe all the telepaths would be nuts. When he thought about it, that didn't seem at all unlikely. He imagined himself with a talent nobody would believe he had.

A thing like that, he told himself glumly, could drive you buggy in short order—and then where were you?

In a loony bin, that's where you were.

Or, possibly, in Yucca Flats. Malone pictured the scene: there they would be, just one big happy family. Kenneth J. Malone, and a convention of bats straight out of the nation's foremost loony bins.

Fun!

Malone began to wonder why he had gone into FBI work in the first place.

"Listen, Chief," he said. "I—"

"Sure, I understand," Burris said quickly. "She's batty. And this new one is batty, too. But what else can we do? Malone, don't do anything you'll regret."

"Regret?" Malone said. "Like what?"

"I mean, don't resign."

"Chief, how did you know—you're not telepathic too, are you?"

"Of course not," Burris said. "But that's what I'd do in your place."

"Well—"

"Remember, Malone," Burris said. His face took on a stern, stuffed expression. "Do not ask what your country can do for you," he quoted the youngest living ex-President. "Ask rather what you can do for your country."

"Sure," Malone said sadly.

"Well, it's true, isn't it?" Burris asked.

"What if it is?" Malone said. "It's still terrible. Everything is terrible. Look at the situation."

"I am looking," Burris said. "And it's another New Frontier. Just like it was when President Kennedy first said those words."

"A New Frontier inhabited entirely by maniacs," Malone said. "Perfectly wonderful. What a way to run a world."

"That," Burris said, "is the way the ball bounces. Or whatever you're supposed to say. Malone, don't think you haven't got my sympathy. You have. I know how hard the job is you're doing."

"You couldn't," Malone told him bitterly.

"Well, anyhow," Burris went on, "don't resign. Stay on the job. Don't give it up, Malone. Don't desert the ship. I want you to promise me you won't do it."

"Look, chief," Malone said. "These nuts—"

"Malone, you've done a wonderful job so far," Burris said. "You'll get a raise and a better job when all this is over. Who else would have thought of looking in the twitch-bins for telepaths? But you did, Malone, and I'm proud of you, and you're stuck with it. We've got to use them now. We have to find that spy!" He took a breath. "On to Yucca Flats!" he said.

Malone gave up. "Yes, sir," he said. "Anything else?"

"Not right now," Burris said. "If there is, I'll let you know."

Malone hung up unhappily as the image vanished. He looked across at Dr. Harman. "Well," he said, "that's that. What do I have to do to get a release for Miss Thompson?"

Harman stared at him. "But, Mr. Malone," he said, "that just isn't possible. Really. Miss Thompson is a ward of the state, and we couldn't possibly allow her release without a court order."

Malone thought that over. "Okay," he said at last. "I can see that." He turned to Boyd. "Here's a job for you,

Tom," he said. "Get one of the judges on the phone. You'll know which one will do us the most good, fastest."

"Mmm," Boyd said. "Say Judge Dunning," he said. "Good man. Fast worker."

"I don't care who," Malone said. "Just get going, and get us a release for Miss Thompson." He turned back to the doctor. "By the way," he said. "Has she got any other name? Besides Elizabeth Tudor, I mean," he added hurriedly.

"Her full name," Dr. Harman said, "is Rose Walker Thompson. She is not Queen Elizabeth I, II or XXVIII, and she is not immortal."

"But she is," Malone pointed out, "a telepath. And that's why I want her."

"She may," Dr. Harman said, "be a telepath." It was obvious that he had partly managed to forget the disturbing incidents that had happened a few minutes before. "I don't even want to discuss that part of it."

"Okay, never mind it," Malone said agreeably. "Tom, get us a court order for Rose Walker Thompson. Effective yesterday—day before, if possible."

Boyd nodded, but before he could get to the phone Dr. Harman spoke again.

"Now, wait a moment, gentlemen," he said. "Court order or no court order, Miss Thompson is definitely not a well woman, and I can't see my way clear to—"

"I'm not well myself," Malone said. "I need sleep and I probably have a cold. But I've got to work for the national security, and—"

"This is important," Boyd put in.

"I don't dispute that," Dr. Harman said. "Nevertheless, I—"

The door that led into the other room burst suddenly open. The three men turned to stare at Miss Wilson, who stood in the doorway for a long second and then stepped into the office, closing the door quietly behind her.

"I'm sorry to interrupt," she said.

"Not at all," Malone said. "It's a pleasure to have you. Come again soon." He smiled at her.

She didn't smile back. "Doctor," she said, "you'd really

better talk to Miss Thompson. I'm not at all sure what I can do. It's something new."

"New?" he said. The worry lines on his face were increasing, but he spoke softly.

"The poor dear thinks she's going to get out of the hospital now," Miss Wilson said. "For some reason, she's convinced that the FBI is going to get her released, and—"

As she saw the expression on three faces, she stopped.

"What's wrong?" she said.

"Miss Wilson," Malone said, "we—may I call you by your first name?"

"Of course, Mr. Malone," she said.

There was a little silence.

"Miss Wilson," Malone said, "what *is* your first name?"

She smiled now, very gently. Malone wanted to walk through mountains, or climb fire. He felt confused, but wonderful. "Barbara," she said.

"Lovely," he said. "Well, Barbara—and please call me Ken. It's short for Kenneth."

The smile on her face broadened. "I thought it might be," she said.

"Well," Malone said softly, "it is. Kenneth. That's my name. And you're Barbara."

Boyd cleared his throat.

"Ah," Malone said. "Yes. Of course. Well, Barbara—well, that's just what we intend to do. Take Miss Thompson away. We need her—badly."

Dr. Harman had said nothing at all, and had barely moved. He was staring at a point on his desk. "She couldn't possibly have heard us," he muttered. "That's a soundproof door. She couldn't have heard us."

"But you can't take Miss Thompson away," Miss Wilson said.

"We have to, Barbara," Malone said gently. "Try to understand. It's for the national security."

"She heard us thinking," Dr. Harman muttered. "That's what; she heard us thinking. Behind a soundproof door. She can see inside their minds. She can even see inside *my* mind."

"She's a sick woman," Barbara said.

"But you have to understand—"

"Vital necessity," Boyd put in. "Absolutely vital."

"Nevertheless—" Barbara said.

"She can read minds," Dr. Harman whispered in an awed tone. "She knows. Everything. She *knows*."

"It's out of the question," Barbara said. "Whether you like it or not, Miss Thompson is not going to leave this hospital. Why, what could she do outside these walls? She hasn't left in over forty years! And furthermore, Mr. Malone—"

"Kenneth," Malone put in, as the door opened again. "I mean Ken."

The little old lady put her haloed head into the room. "Now, now, Barbara," she said. "Don't you go spoiling things. Just let these nice men take me away and everything will be fine, believe me. Besides, I've been outside more often then you imagine."

"Outside?" Barbara said.

"Of course," the little old lady said. "In other people's minds. Even yours. I remember that nice young man—what was his name?—"

"Never mind his name," Barbara said, flushing furiously.

Malone felt instantly jealous of every nice young man he had ever even heard of. *He* wasn't a nice young man; he was an FBI agent, and he liked to get drunk and smoke cigars and carouse with loose women. Anyway, reasonably loose women.

All nice young men, he decided, should be turned into ugly old men as soon as possible. That'll fix them!

He noticed the little old lady smiling at him, and tried to change his thoughts rapidly. But the little old lady said nothing at all.

"At any rate," Barbara said, "I'm afrad that we just can't—"

Dr. Harman cleared his throat imperiously. It was a most impressive noise, and everyone turned to look at him. His face was a little gray, but he looked, otherwise, like a rather pudgy, blond, crew-cut Roman emperor.

"Just a moment," he said with dignity. "I think you're doing the United States of America a grave injustice,

Miss Wilson—and that you're doing an injustice to Miss Thompson, too."

"What do you mean?" she said.

"I think it would be nice for her to get away from me —I mean from here," the psychiatrist said. "Where did you say you were taking her?" he asked Malone.

"Yucca Flats," Malone said.

"Ah." The news seemed to please the psychiatrist. "That's a long distance from here, isn't it? It's quite a few hundred miles away. Perhaps even a few thousand miles away. I feel sure that will be the best thing for me—I mean, of course, for Miss Thompson. I shall recommend that the court so order."

"Doctor—" But even Barbara saw, Malone could tell, that it was no good arguing with Dr. Harman. She tried a last attack. "Doctor, who's going to take care of her?"

A light the size and shape of North America burst in Malone's mind. He almost chortled. But he managed to keep his voice under control. "What she needs," he said, "is a trained psychiatric nurse."

Barbara Wilson gave him a look that had carloads of U$_{235}$ stacked away in it, but Malone barely minded. She'd get over it, he told himself.

"Now, wasn't that sweet of you to think of that," the little old lady said. Malone looked at her and was rewarded with another wink. *Good God,* he thought. *She reads minds!*

"I'm certainly glad you thought of Barbara," the little old lady went on. "You will go with me, won't you, dear? I'll make you a duchess. Wouldn't you like to be a duchess, dear?"

Barbara looked from Malone to the little old lady, and then she looked at Dr. Harman. Apparently what she saw failed to make her happy.

"We'll take good care of her, Barbara," Malone said.

She didn't even bother to give him an answer. After a second Boyd said: "Well, I guess that settles it. If you'll let me use your phone, Dr. Harman, I'll call Judge Dunning."

"Go right ahead," Dr. Harman said. "Go right ahead."

The little old lady smiled softly without looking at anybody at all. "Won't it be wonderful," she whispered. "At last I've been recognized. My country is about to pay me for my services. My loyal subjects . . ." She stopped and wiped what Malone thought was a tear from one cornflower-blue eye.

"Now, now, Miss Thompson," Barbara said.

"I'm not sad," the little old lady said, smiling up at her. "I'm just so very happy. I am about to get my reward, my well-deserved reward at last, from all of my loyal subjects. You'll see." She paused and Malone felt a faint stirring of stark, chill fear.

"Won't it be wonderful?" said the little old lady.

4

"You're *where?*" Andrew J. Burris said.

Malone looked at the surprised face on the screen and wished he hadn't called. He had to report in, of course —but, if he'd had any sense, he'd have ordered Boyd to do the job for him.

Oh, well, it was too late for that now. "I'm in Las Vegas," he said. "I tried to get you last night, but I couldn't, so I—"

"Las Vegas," Burris said. "Well, well. Las Vegas." His face darkened and his voice became very loud. "Why aren't you in Yucca Flats?" he screamed.

"Because she insisted on it," Malone said. "The old lady. Miss Thompson. She says there's another telepath here."

Burris closed his eyes. "Well, that's a relief," he said at last. "Somebody in one of the gambling houses, I suppose. Fine, Malone." He went right on without a pause: "The boys have uncovered two more in various parts of the nation. Not one of them is even close to sane." He opened his eyes. "Where's this one?" he said.

Malone sighed. "In the looney bin," he said.

Burris' eyes closed again. Malone waited in silence. At last Burris said: "All right. Get him out."

"Right," Malone said.

"Tell me," Burris said. "Why did Miss Thompson insist that you go to Las Vegas? Somebody else could have done the job. You could have sent Boyd, couldn't you?"

"Chief," Malone said slowly, "what sort of mental condition are those other telepaths in?"

"Pretty bad," Burris said. "As a matter of fact, very bad. Miss Thompson may be off her trolley, but the others haven't even got any tracks." He paused. "What's that got to do with it?" he said.

"Well," Malone said, "I figured we'd better handle Miss Thompson with kid gloves—at least until we find a better telepath to work with." He didn't mention Barbara Wilson. The chief, he told himself, didn't want to be bothered with details.

"Doggone right you'd better," Burris said. "You treat that old lady as if she were the Queen herself, understand?"

"Don't worry," Malone said unhappily. "We are." He hesitated. "She says she'll help us find our spy, all right, but we've got to do it her way—or else she won't cooperate."

"Do it her way, then," Burris said. "That spy—"

"Chief, are you sure?"

Burris blinked. "Well, then," he said, "what *is* her way?"

Malone took a deep breath. "First," he said, "we had to come here and pick this guy up. This William Logan, who's in a private sanitarium just ouside of Las Vegas. That's number one. Miss Thompson wants to get all the telepaths together, so they can hold mental conversations or something."

"And all of them batty," Burris said.

"Sure," Malone said. "A convention of nuts—and me in the middle. Listen, Chief—"

"Later," Burris said. "When this is over we can all resign, or go fishing, or just plain shoot ourselves. But right now the national security is primary, Malone. Remember that."

"Okay," Malone sighed. "Okay. But she wants all the nuts here."

"Go along with her," Burris snapped. "Keep her happy. So far, Malone, she's the only lead we have on the guy who's swiping information from Yucca Flats. If she wants something, Malone, you do it."

"But, Chief—"

"Don't interrupt me," Burris said. "If she wants to be treated like a Queen, you treat her like one. Malone, that's an order!"

"Yes, sir," Malone said sadly. "But, Chief, she wants us to buy her some new clothes."

"My God," Burris exploded. "Is that all? New clothes? Get 'em. Put 'em on the expense account. New clothes are a drop in the bucket."

"Well—she thinks we need new clothes, too."

"Maybe you do," Burris said. "Put the whole thing on the expense account. You don't think I'm going to quibble about a few dollars, do you?"

"Well—"

"Get the clothes. Just don't bother me with details like this. Handle the job yourself, Malone—you're in charge out there. And get to Yucca Flats as soon as possible."

Malone gave up. "Yes, sir," he said.

"All right, then," Burris said. "Call me tomorrow. Meanwhile—good luck, Malone. Chin up."

Malone said: "Yes, sir," and reached for the switch. But Burris' voice stopped him.

"Just one thing," he said.

"Yes, Chief?" Malone said.

Burris frowned. "Don't spend any more for the clothes than you have to," he said.

Malone nodded, and cut off.

When the Director's image had vanished, he got up and went to the window of the hotel room. Outside, a huge sign told the world, and Malone, that this was the Thunderbird-Hilton-Zeckendorf Hotel, but Malone ignored it. He didn't need a sign; he knew where he was.

In hot water, he thought. *That's* where he was.

Behind him, the door opened. Malone turned as Boyd came in.

"I found a costume shop, Ken," he said.

"Great," Malone said. "The Chief authorized it."

"He did?" Boyd's round face fell at the news.

"He said to buy her whatever she wants. He says to treat her like a Queen."

"That," Boyd said, "we're doing now."

"I know it," Malone said. "I know it altogether too well."

"Anyhow," Boyd said, brightening, "the costume shop doesn't do us any good. They've only got cowboy stuff and bullfighters' costumes and Mexican stuff—you know, for their Helldorado Week here."

"You didn't give up, did you?" Malone said.

Boyd shook his head. "Of course not," he said. "Ken: this is on the expense account, isn't it?"

"Expense account," Malone said. "Sure it is."

Boyd looked relieved. "Good," he said. "Because I had the proprietor phone her size in, to New York."

"Better get two of 'em," Malone said. "The Chief said anything she wanted, she was supposed to have."

"I'll go back right away. I told him we wanted the stuff on the afternoon plane, so—"

"And give him Bar—Miss Wilson's size, and yours, and mine. Tell him to dig up something appropriate."

"For us?" Boyd blanched visibly.

"For us," Malone said grimly.

Boyd set his jaw. "No," he said.

"Listen, Tom," Malone said, "I don't like this any better than you do. But if I can't resign, you can't either. Costumes for everybody."

"But," Boyd said, and stopped. After a second he went on: "Malone—Ken—FBI agents are supposed to be inconspicuous, aren't they?"

Malone nodded.

"Well, how inconspicuous are we going to be in this stuff?"

"It's an idea," Malone said. "But it isn't a very good one. Our first job is to keep Miss Thompson happy. And that means costumes."

Boyd said: "My God."

"And what's more," Malone added, "from now on she's 'Your Majesty.' Got that?"

"Ken," Boyd said, "you've gone nuts."

Malone shook his head. "No, I haven't," he said. "I just wish I had. It would be a relief."

"Me too," Boyd said. He started for the door and turned. "I wish I could have stayed in San Francisco," he said. "Why should she insist on taking *me* along?"

"The beard," Malone said.

"*My* beard?" Boyd recoiled.

"Right," Malone said. "She says it reminds her of someone she knows. Frankly, it reminds me of someone, too. Only I don't know who."

Boyd gulped. "I'll shave it off," he said, with the air of a man who can do no more to propitiate the Gods.

"You will not," Malone said firmly. "Touch but a hair of yon black chin, and I'll peel off your entire skin."

Boyd winced.

"Now," Malone said, "go back to that costume shop and arrange things. Here." He fished in his pockets and came out with a crumpled slip of paper and handed it to Boyd. "That's a list of my clothing sizes. Get another list from B—Miss Wilson." Boyd nodded. Malone thought he detected a strange glint in the other man's eye. "Don't measure her yourself," he said. "Just ask her."

Boyd scratched his bearded chin and nodded slowly. "All right, Ken," he said. "But if we just don't get anywhere, don't blame me."

"If you get anywhere," Malone said, "I'll snatch you baldheaded. And I'll leave the beard."

"I didn't mean with Miss Wilson, Ken," Boyd said. "I

meant in general." He left, with the air of a man whose world has betrayed him. His back looked, to Malone, like the back of a man on his way to the scaffold or guillotine.

The door closed.

Now, Malone thought, who does that beard remind me of? Who do I know who knows Miss Thompson?

And what difference does it make?

Nevertheless, he told himself, Boyd's beard (Beard's boyd?) was really an admirable fact of nature. Ever since beards had become popular again in the mid-sixties, and FBI agents had been permitted to wear them, Malone had thought about growing one. But, somehow, it didn't seem right.

Now, looking at Boyd, he began to think about the prospect again.

He shrugged the notion away. There were things to do.

He picked up the phone and called Information.

"Can you give me," he said, "the number of the Desert Edge Sanatorium?"

The crimson blob of the setting sun was already painting the desert sky with its customary purples and oranges by the time the little caravan arrived at the Desert Edge Sanatorium, a square white building several miles out of Las Vegas. Malone, in the first car, wondered briefly about the kind of patients they catered to. People driven mad by vingt-et-un or poker-dice? Neurotic chorus ponies? Gambling czars with delusions of non-persecution?

Sitting in the front seat next to Boyd, he watched the unhappy San Francisco agent manipulating the wheel. In the back seat, Queen Elizabeth Thompson and Lady Barbara, the nurse, were located, and Her Majesty was chattering away like a magpie.

Malone eyed the rearview mirror to get a look at the car following them and the two local FBI agents in it. They were, he thought, unbelievably lucky. He had to sit and listen to the Royal Personage in the back seat.

"Of course, as soon as Parliament convenes and recognizes me," she was saying, "I shall confer personages on all of you. Right now, the best I could do was to knight you all, and of course that's hardly enough. But I think I shall make Sir Kenneth the Duke of Columbia."

Sir Kenneth, Malone realized, was himself. He wondered how he'd like being Duke of Columbia—and wouldn't the President be surprised!

"And Sir Thomas," the Queen continued, "will be the Duke of—what? Sir Thomas?"

"Yes, Your Majesty?" Boyd said, trying to sound both eager and properly respectful.

"What would you like to be Duke of?" she said.

"Oh," Boyd said after a second's thought, "anything that pleases Your Majesty." But apparently, his thoughts gave him away.

"You're from upstate New York?" the Queen said. "How very nice. Then you must be made the Duke of Poughkeepsie."

"Thank you, Your Majesty," Boyd said. Malone thought he detected a note of pride in the man's voice, and shot a glance at Boyd, but the agent was driving with a serene face and an economy of motion.

Duke of Poughkeepsie! Malone thought. *Hah!*

He leaned back and adjusted his fur-trimmed coat. The plume that fell from his cap kept tickling his neck, and he brushed at it without success.

All four of the inhabitants of the car were dressed in late Sixteenth Century costumes, complete with ruffs and velvet and lace filigree. Her Majesty and Lady Barbara were wearing the full skirts and small skullcaps of the era (and on Barbara, Malone thought privately, the low-cut gowns didn't look at all disappointing), and Sir Thomas and Malone (Sir Kenneth, he thought sourly) were clad in doublet, hose and long coats with fur trim and slashed sleeves. And all of them were loaded down, weighted down, staggeringly, with gems.

Naturally, the gems were fake. But then, Malone thought, the Queen was mad. It all balanced out in the end.

As they approached the sanitarium, Malone breathed

a thankful prayer that he'd called up to tell the head physician how they'd all be dressed. If he hadn't . . .

He didn't want to think about that.

He didn't even want to pass it by hurriedly on a dark night.

The head physician, Dr. Frederic Dowson, was waiting for them on the steps of the building. He was a tall, thin, cadaverous-looking man with almost no hair and very deep-sunken eyes. He had the kind of face that a gushing female would probably describe, Malone thought, as "craggy," but it didn't look in the least attractive to Malone. Instead, it looked tough and forbidding.

He didn't turn a hair as the magnificently robed Boyd slid from the front seat, opened the rear door, doffed his plumed hat, and in one low sweep made a great bow. "We are here, Your Majesty," Boyd said.

Her Majesty got out, clutching at her voluminous skirts in a worried manner, to keep from catching them on the door-jamb. "You know, Sir Thomas," she said when she was standing free of the car, "I think we must be related."

"Ah?" Boyd said worriedly.

"I'm certain of it, in fact," Her Majesty went on. "You look just exactly like my poor father. Just exactly. I dare say you come from one of the sinister branches of the family. Perhaps you are a half-brother of mine—removed, of course."

Malone grinned, and tried to hide the expression. Boyd was looking puzzled, then distantly angered. Nobody had ever called him illegitimate in just that way before.

But Her Majesty was absolutely right, Malone thought. The agent had always reminded him of someone, and now, at last, he knew exactly who. The hair hadn't been black, either, but red.

Boyd was, in Elizabethan costume, the deadest of dead ringers for Henry VIII.

Malone went up the steps to where Dr. Dowson was standing.

"I'm Malone," he said, checking a tendency to bow. "I called earlier today. Is this William Logan of yours ready to go? We can take him back with us in the second car."

Dr. Dowson compressed his lips and looked worried. "Come in, Mr. Malone," he said. He turned just as the second carload of FBI agents began emptying itself over the hospital grounds.

The entire procession filed into the hospital office, the two local agents following up the rear. Since they were not a part of Her Majesty's personal retinue, they had not been required to wear court costumes. In a way, Malone was beginning to feel sorry for them. He himself cut a nice figure in the outfit, he thought— rather like Errol Flynn in the old black-and-white print of *The Prince and the Pauper*.

But there was no denying that the procession looked strange. File clerks and receptionists stopped their work to gape at the four bedizened walkers and their plainly dressed satellites. Malone needed no telepathic talent to tell what they were thinking.

"A whole roundup of nuts," they were thinking. "And those two fellows in the back must be bringing them in —along with Dr. Dowson."

Malone straightened his spine. Really, he didn't see why Elizabethan costumes had ever gone out of style. Elizabeth was back, wasn't she—either Elizabeth II, on the throne, or Elizabeth I, right behind him. Either way you looked at it . . .

When they were all inside the waiting room, Dr. Dowson said: "Now, Mr. Malone, just what is all this about?" He rubbed his long hands together. "I fail to see the humor of the situation."

"Humor?" Malone said.

"Doctor," Barbara Wilson began, "let me explain. You see—"

"These ridiculous costumes," Dr. Dowson said, waving a hand at them. "You may feel that poking fun at insanity is humorous, Mr. Malone, but let me tell you—"

"It wasn't like that at all," Boyd said.

"And," Dr. Dowson continued in a somewhat louder voice, "wanting to take Mr. Logan away from us. Mr.

Logan is a very sick man, Mr. Malone. He should be properly cared for."

"I promise we'll take good care of him," Malone said earnestly. The Elizabethan clothes were fine outdoors, but in a heated room one had a tendency to sweat.

"I take leave to doubt that," Dr. Dowson said, eyeing their costumes pointedly.

"Miss Wilson here," Malone volunteered, "is a trained psychiatric nurse."

Barbara, in her gown, stepped forward. "Dr. Dowson," she said, "let me assure you that these costumes have their purpose. We—"

"Not only that," Malone said. "There are a group of trained men from St. Elizabeths Hospital in Washington who are going to take the best of care of him." He said nothing whatever about Yucca Flats, or about telepathy.

Why spread around information unnecessarily?

"But I don't understand," Dr. Dowson said. "What interest could the FBI have in an insane man?"

"That's none of your business," Malone said. He reached inside his fur-trimmed robe and, again suppressing a tendency to bow deeply, withdrew an impressive-looking legal document. "This," he said, "is a court order, instructing you to hand over to us the person of one William Logan, herein identified and described." He waved it at the Doctor. "That's your William Logan," he said, "only now he's ours."

Dr. Dowson took the papers and put in some time frowning at them. Then he looked up again at Malone. "I assume that I have some discretion in this matter," he said. "And I wonder if you realize just how ill Mr. Logan is? We have his case histories here, and we have worked with him for some time."

Barbara Wilson said: "But—"

"I might say that we are begining to understand his illness," Dr. Dowson said. "I honestly don't think it would be proper to transfer this work to another group of therapists. It might set his illness back—cause, as it were, a relapse. All our work could easily be nullified."

"Please, Doctor," Barbara Wilson began.

"I'm afraid the court order's got to stand," Malone

said. Privately, he felt sorry for Dr. Dowson, who was, obviously enough, a conscientious man trying to do the best he could for his patient. But—

"I'm sorry, Dr. Dowson," he said. "We'll expect that you send all of your data to the government psychiatrists —and, naturally, any concern for the patient's welfare will be our concern also. The FBI isn't anxious for its workers to get the reputation of careless men." He paused, wondering what other bone he could throw the man. "I have no doubt that the St. Elizabeths men will be happy to accept your cooperation," he said at last. "But, I'm afraid that our duty is clear. William Logan goes with us."

Dr. Dowson looked at them sourly. "Does he have to get dressed up like a masquerade, too?" Before Malone could answer, the psychiatrist added: "Anyhow, I don't even know you're FBI men. After all, why should I comply with orders from a group of men, dressed insanely, whom I don't even know?"

Malone didn't say anything. He just got up and walked to a phone on a small table, near the wall. Next to it was a door, and Malone wondered uncomfortably what was behind it. Maybe Dr. Dowson had a small arsenal there, to protect his patients and prevent people from pirating them.

He looked back at the set and dialled Burris' private number in Washington. When the Director's face appeared on the screen, Malone said: "Mr. Burris, will you please identify me to Dr. Dowson?" He looked over at Dowson. "You recognize Mr. Andrew J. Burris, I suppose?" he said.

Dowson nodded. His grim face showed a faint shock. He walked to the phone, and Malone stepped back to let him talk with Burris.

"My name is Dowson," he said. "I'm psychiatric director here at Desert Edge Sanatorium. And your men—"

"My men have orders to take William Logan from your care," Burris said.

"That's right," Dowson said. "But—"

While they were talking, Queen Elizabeth I sidled

quietly up to Malone and tapped him on the shoulder.

"Sir Kenneth," she whispered in the faintest of voices, "I know where your telepathic spy is. And I know *who* he is."

"Who?" Malone said. "What? Why? Where?" He blinked and whirled. It couldn't be true. They couldn't solve the case so easily.

But the Queen's face was full of a majestic assurance. "He's right there," she said, and she pointed.

Malone followed her finger.

It was aimed directly at the glowing image of Andrew J. Burris, Director of the FBI.

5

Malone opened his mouth, but nothing came out. Not even air.

He wasn't breathing.

He stared at Burris for a long moment, then took a breath and looked again at Her Majesty. "The spy?" he whispered.

"That's right," she said.

"But that's—" He had to fight for control. "That's the head of the FBI," he mananged to say. "Do you mean to say he's a spy?"

Burris was saying: ". . . I'm afraid this is a matter of

importance, Dr. Dowson. We cannot tolerate delay. You have the court order. Obey it."

"Very well, Mr. Burris," Dowson said with an obvious lack of grace. "I'll release him to Mr. Malone immediately, since you insist."

Malone stared, fascinated. Then he turned back to the little old lady. "Do you mean to tell me," he said, "that Andrew J. Burris is a telepathic spy?"

"Oh, dear me," Her Majesty said, obviously aghast. "My goodness gracious. Is that Mr. Burris on the screen?"

"It is," Malone assured her. A look out of the corner of his eye told him that neither Burris, in Washington, nor Dowson or any others in the room, had heard any of the conversation. Malone lowered his whisper some more, just in case. "That's the head of the FBI," he said.

"Well, then," Her Majesty said, "Mr. Burris couldn't possibly be a spy, then, could he? Not if he's the head of the FBI. Of course not. Mr. Burris simply isn't a spy. He isn't the type. Forget all about Mr. Burris."

"I can't," Malone said at random. "I work for him." He closed his eyes. The room, he had discovered, was spinning slightly. "Now," he said, "you're sure he's not a spy?"

"Certainly I'm sure," she said, with her most regal tones. "Do you doubt the word of your sovereign?"

"Not exactly," Malone said. Truthfully, he wasn't at all sure. Not at all. But why tell that to the Queen?

"Shame on you," she said. "You shouldn't even think such things. After all, I am the Queen, aren't I?" But there was a sweet, gentle smile on her face when she spoke; she didn't seem to be really irritated.

"Sure you are," Malone said. "But—"

"Malone!" It was Burris' voice, from the phone. Malone spun around. "Take Mr. Logan," Burris said, "and get going. There's been enough delay as it is."

"Yes, sir," Malone said. "Right away, sir. Anything else?"

"That's all," Burris said. "Good night." The screen blanked.

There was a little silence.

"All right, Doctor," Boyd said. He looked every inch

a king, and Malone knew exactly what king. "Bring him out."

Dr. Dowson heaved a great sigh. "Very well," he said heavily. "But I want it known that I resent this highhanded treatment, and I shall write a letter complaining of it." He pressed a button on an instrument panel in his desk. "Bring Mr. Logan in," he said.

Malone wasn't in the least worried about the letter. Burris, he knew, would take care of anything like that. And, besides, he had other things to think about.

The door to the next room had opened almost immediately, and two husky, white-clad men were bringing in a strait-jacketed figure whose arms were wrapped against his chest, while the jacket's extra-long sleeves were tied behind his back. He walked where the attendants led him, but his eyes weren't looking at anything in the room. They stared at something far away and invisible, an impalpable shifting nothingness somewhere in the infinite distances beyond the world.

For the first time, Malone felt the chill of panic. Here, he thought, was insanity of a very real and frightening kind. Queen Elizabeth Thompson was one thing—and she was almost funny, and likeable, after all. But William Logan was something else, and something that sent a wave of cold shivering into the room.

What made it worse was that Logan wasn't a man, but a boy, barely nineteen. Malone had known that, of course—but seeing it was something different. The lanky, awkward figure wrapped in a hospital strait-jacket was horrible, and the smooth, unconcerned face was, somehow, worse. There was no threat in that face, no terror or anger or fear. It was merely—a blank.

It was not a human face. Its complete lack of emotion or expression could have belonged to a sleeping child of ten—or to a member of a different race. Malone looked at the boy, and looked away.

Was it possible that Logan knew what he was thinking?

Answer me, he thought, directly at the still boy.

There was no reply, none at all. Malone forced himself to look away. But the air in the room seemed to have become much colder.

The attendants stood on either side of him, waiting. For one long second no one moved, and then Dr. Dowson reached into his desk drawer and produced a sheaf of papers.

"If you'll sign these for the government," he said, "you may have Mr. Logan. There seems little else that I can do, Mr. Malone—in spite of my earnest pleas—"

"I'm sorry," Malone said. After all, he *needed* Logan, didn't he? After a look at the boy, he wasn't sure any more—but the Queen had said she wanted him, and the Queen's word was law. Or what passed for law, anyhow, at least for the moment.

Malone took the papers and looked them over. There was nothing special about them; they were merely standard release forms, absolving the staff and management of Desert Edge Sanatorium from every conceivable responsibility under any conceivable circumstances, as far as William Logan was concerned. Dr. Dowson gave Malone a look that said: "Very well, Mr. Malone; I will play Pilate and wash my hands of the matter—but you needn't think I like it." It was a lot for one look to say, but Dr. Dowson's dark and sunken eyes got the message across with no loss in transmission. As a matter of fact, there seemed to be more coming—a much less printable message was apparently on the way through those glittering, sad and angry eyes.

Malone avoided them nervously, and went over the papers again instead. At last he signed them and handed them back. "Thanks for your cooperation, Dr. Dowson," he said briskly, feeling ten kinds of a traitor.

"Not at all," Dowson said bitterly. "Mr. Logan is now in your custody. I must trust you to take good care of him."

"The best care we can," Malone said. It didn't seem sufficient. He added: "The best possible care, Doctor," and tried to look dependable and trustworthy, like a Boy Scout. He was aware that the effort failed miserably.

At his signal, the two plainclothes FBI men took over from the attendants. They marched Logan out to their car, and Malone led the procession back to Boyd's automobile, a procession that consisted (in order) of Sir

Kenneth Malone, prospective Duke of Columbia, Queen Elizabeth I, Lady Barbara, prospective Duchess of an unspecified county, and Sir Thomas Boyd, prospective Duke of Poughkeepsie. Malone hummed a little of the first *Pomp and Circumstance* march as they walked; somehow, he thought it was called for.

They piled into the car, Boyd at the wheel with Malone next to him, and the two ladies in back, with Queen Elizabeth sitting directly behind Sir Thomas. Boyd started the engine and they turned and roared off.

"Well," said Her Majesty with an air of great complacence, "that's that. That makes six of us."

Malone looked around the car. He counted the people. There were four. He said, puzzled: "Six?"

"That's right, Sir Kenneth," Her Majesty said. "You have it exactly. Six."

"You mean six telepaths?" Sir Thomas asked in a deferent tone of voice.

"Certainly I do," Her Majesty replied. "We telepaths, you know, must stick together. That's the reason I got poor little Willie out of that sanatorium of his, you know —and, of course, the others will be joining us."

"Don't you think it's time for your nap, dear?" Lady Barbara put in suddenly.

"My *what?*" It was obvious that Queen Elizabeth was Not Amused.

"Your nap, dear," Lady Barbara said.

"Don't call me dear," Her Majesty snapped.

"I'm sorry, Your Majesty," Barbara murmured. "But really—"

"My dear girl," Her Majesty said, "I am not a child. I am your sovereign. Do try to have a little respect. Why, I remember when Shakespeare used to say to me—but that's no matter, not now."

"About those telepaths—" Boyd began.

"Telepaths," Her Majesty said. "Ah, yes. We must all stick together. In the hospital, you know, we had a little joke—the patients for Insulin Shock Therapy used to say: 'If we don't stick together, we'll all be stuck separately.' Do you see, Sir Thomas?"

"But," Sir Kenneth Malone said, trying desperately to

return to the point. *"Six?"* He had counted them up in his mind. Burris had mentioned one found in St. Elizabeths, and two more picked up later. With Queen Elizabeth, and now William Logan, that made five.

Unless the Queen was counting him in. There didn't seem any good reason why not.

"Oh, no," Her Majesty said with a little trill of laughter, "not you, Sir Kenneth. I meant Mr. Miles."

Sir Thomas Boyd asked: "Mr. Miles?"

"That's right," Her Majesty said. "His name is Barry Miles, and your FBI men found him an hour ago in New Orleans. They're bringing him to Yucca Flats to meet the rest of us; isn't that nice?"

Lady Barbara cleared her throat.

"It really isn't necessary for you to try to get my attention, dear," the Queen said. "After all, I do know what you're thinking."

Lady Barbara blinked. "I still want to suggest, respectfully, about that nap—" she began.

"My dear girl," the Queen said, with the faintest trace of impatience, "I do not feel the least bit tired, and this is such an exciting day that I just don't want to miss any of it. Besides, I've already told you I don't want a nap. It isn't polite to be insistent to your Queen—no matter how strongly you feel about a matter. I'm sure you'll learn to understand that, dear."

Lady Barbara opened her mouth, shut it again, and opened it once more. "My goodness," she said.

"That's the idea," Her Majesty said approvingly. "Think before you speak—and then don't speak. It really isn't necessary, since I know what you're thinking."

Malone said grimly: "About this new telepath—this Barry Miles. Did they find him—"

"In a nut-house?" Her Majesty said sweetly. "Why, of course, Sir Kenneth. You were quite right when you thought that telepaths went insane because they had a sense they couldn't effectively use, and because no one believed them. How would you feel, if nobody believed you could see?"

"Strange," Malone admitted.

"There," Her Majesty said. "You see? Telepaths do

go insane—it's sort of an occupational disease. Of course, not all of them are insane."

"Not all of them?" Malone felt the faint stirrings of hope. Perhaps they would turn up a telepath yet who was completely sane and rational.

"There's me, of course," Her Majesty said.

Lady Barbara gulped audibly. Boyd said nothing, but gripped the wheel of the car more tightly.

And Malone thought to himself: *That's right. There's Queen Elizabeth—who says she isn't crazy.*

And then he thought of one more sane telepath. But the knowledge didn't make him feel any better.

It was, of course, the spy.

How many more are going to turn up? Malone wondered.

"Oh, that's about all of us," the Queen said. "There is one more, but she's in a hospital in Honolulu, and your men won't find her until tomorrow."

Boyd turned. "Do you mean you can foretell the future, too?" he asked in a strained voice.

Lady Barbara screamed: "Keep your eyes on the wheel and your hands on the road!"

"What?" Boyd said.

There was a terrific blast of noise, and a truck went by in the opposite direction. The driver, a big, ugly man with no hair on his head, leaned out to curse at the quartet, but his mouth remained open. He stared at the four Elizabethans and said nothing at all as he whizzed by.

"What was that?" Boyd asked faintly.

"That," Malone snapped, "was a truck. And it was due entirely to the mercy of God that we didn't hit it. Barbara's right. Keep your eyes on the wheel and your hands on the road." He paused and thought that over. Then he said: "Does that mean anything at all?"

"Lady Barbara was confused by the excitement," the Queen said calmly. "It's all right now, dear."

Lady Barbara blinked across the seat. "I was—afraid," she said.

"It's all right," the Queen said. "I'll take care of you."

89

"This," Malone announced to no one in particular, "is ridiculous."

Boyd swept the car around a curve and concentrated grimly on the road. After a second the Queen said: "Since you're still thinking about the question, I'll answer you."

"What question?" Malone said, thoroughly baffled.

"Sir Thomas asked me if I could foretell the future," the Queen said equably. "Of course I can't. That's silly. Just because I'm immortal and I'm a telepath, don't go hog-wild."

"Then how did you know the FBI agents were going to find the girl in Honolulu tomorrow?" Boyd said.

"Because," the Queen said, "they're thinking about looking in the hospital tomorrow, and when they look they'll certainly find her."

Boyd said: "Oh," and was silent.

But Malone had a grim question. "Why didn't you tell me about these other telepaths before?" he said. "You could have saved us a lot of work."

"Oh, heavens to Betsy, Sir Kenneth," Her Majesty exclaimed. "How could I? After all, the proper precautions had to be taken first, didn't they? I told you all the others were crazy—*really* crazy, I mean. And they just wouldn't be safe without the proper precautions."

"Perhaps you ought to go back to the hospital, too," Barbara said, and added: "Your Majesty," just in time.

"But if I did, dear," Her Majesty said, "you'd lose your chance to become a Duchess, and that wouldn't be at all nice. Besides, I'm having so much *fun!*" She trilled a laugh again. "Riding around like this is just wonderful!" she said.

And you're important for national security, Malone said to himself.

"That's right, Sir Kenneth," the Queen said. "The country needs me, and I'm happy to serve. That is the job of a sovereign."

"Fine," Malone said, hoping it was.

"Well, then," said Her Majesty, "that settles that. We have a whole night ahead of us, Sir Kenneth. What do you say we make a night *of* it?"

"Knight who?" Malone said. He felt confused again. It seemed as if he was always feeling confused lately.

"Don't be silly, Sir Kenneth," Her Majesty said. "There are times and times."

"Sure," Malone said at random. *And time and a half,* he thought. *Possibly for overtime.* "What is Your Majesty thinking of?" he asked with trepidation.

"I want to take a tour of Las Vegas," Her Majesty said primly.

Lady Barbara shook her head. "I'm afraid that's not possible, Your Majesty," she said.

"And why not, pray?" Her Majesty said. "No. I can see what you're thinking. It's not safe to let me go wandering around in a strange city, and particularly if that city is Las Vegas. Well, dear, I can assure you that it's perfectly safe."

"We've got work to do," Boyd contributed.

Malone said nothing. He stared bleakly at the hood ornament on the car.

"I have made my wishes known," the Queen said.

Lady Barbara said: "But—"

Boyd, however, knew when to give in. "Yes, Your Majesty," he said.

She smiled graciously at him, and answered Lady Barbara only by a slight lift of her regal eyebrow.

Malone had been thinking about something else. When he was sure he had a firm grip on himself he turned. "Your Majesty, tell me something," he said. "You can read my mind, right?"

"Well, of course, Sir Kenneth," Her Majesty said. "I thought I'd proved that to you. And, as for what you're about to ask—"

"No," Malone said. "Please. Let me ask the questions before you answer them. It's less confusing that way. I'll cheerfully admit that it shouldn't be—but it is. Please?"

"Certainly, Sir Kenneth, if you wish," the Queen said. She folded her hands in her lap and waited quietly.

"Okay," Malone said. "Now, if you can read my mind, then you must know that I don't *really* believe that you are Queen Elizabeth of England. The First, I mean."

"Mr. Malone," Barbara Wilson said suddenly. "I—"

"It's all right, child," the Queen said. "He doesn't disturb me. And I do wish you'd call him Sir Kenneth. That's his title, you know."

"Now that's what I mean," Malone said. "Why do you want us to *act* as if we believe you, when you know we don't?"

"Because that's the way people do act," the Queen said calmly. "Very few people really believe that their so-called superiors *are* superior. Almost none of them do, in fact."

"Now wait a minute," Boyd began.

"No, no, it's quite true," the Queen said, "and, unpleasant as it may be, we must learn to face the truth. That's the path of sanity." Lady Barbara made a strangled noise but Her Majesty continued, unruffled. "Nearly everybody suffers from the silly delusion that he's possibly equal to, but very probably superior to, everybody else—my goodness, where would we be if that were true?"

Malone felt that a comment was called for, and he made one. "Who knows?" he said.

"All the things people do toward their superiors," the Queen said, "are done for social reasons. For instance, Sir Kenneth: you don't realize fully how you feel about Mr. Burris."

"He's a hell of a fine guy," Malone said. "I work for him. He's a good Director of the FBI."

"Of course," the Queen said. "But you believe you could do the job just as well, or perhaps a little better."

"I do not," Malone said angrily.

Her Majesty reserved a dignified silence.

After a while Malone said: "And what if I do?"

"Why, nothing," Her Majesty said. "You don't think Mr. Burris is any smarter or better than you are—but you treat him as if you did. All I am insisting on is the same treatment."

"But if we don't believe—" Boyd began.

"Bless you," Her Majesty said, "I can't help the way you *think,* but, as Queen, I do have some control over the way you *act.*"

Malone thought it over. "You have a point there," he said at last.

Barbara said: "But—"

"Yes, Sir Kenneth," the Queen said, "I do." She seemed to be ignoring Lady Barbara. Perhaps, Malone thought, she was still angry over the nap affair. "It's not that," the Queen said.

"Not what?" Boyd said, thoroughly confused.

"Not the naps," the Queen said.

"What naps?" Boyd said.

Malone said: "I was thinking—"

"Good," Boyd said. "Keep it up. I'm driving. Everything's going to hell around me, but I'm driving."

A red light appeared ahead. Boyd jammed on the brakes with somewhat more than the necessary force, and Malone was thrown forward with a grunt. Behind him there were two ladylike squeals.

Malone struggled upright. "Barbara?" he called. "Are you all right—" Then he remembered the Queen.

"It's all right," Her Majesty said. "I can understand your concern for Lady Barbara." She smiled at Malone as he turned.

Malone gaped at her. Of course she knew what he thought about Barbara; she'd been reading his mind. And, apparently, she was on his side. That was good, even though it made him slightly nervous to think about.

"Now," the Queen said suddenly, "what about tonight?"

"Tonight?"

"Yes, of course," the Queen said. She smiled, and put up a hand to pat at her white hair under the Elizabethan skullcap. "I think I should like to go to the Palace," she said. "After all, isn't that where a Queen should be?"

Boyd said, in a kind of explosion: "London? England?"

"Oh, dear me . . ." the Queen began, and Barbara said:

"I'm afraid that I simply can't allow anything like that. Overseas—"

"I didn't mean overseas, dear," Her Majesty said. "Sir Kenneth, please explain to these people."

The Palace, Malone knew, was more properly known

as the Golden Palace. It was right in Las Vegas—convenient to all sources of money. As a matter of fact, it was one of the biggest gambling houses along the Las Vegas strip, a veritable chaos of wheels, cards, dice, chips and other such devices. Malone explained all this to the others, wondering meanwhile why Miss Thompson wanted to go there.

"Not Miss Thompson, *please,* Sir Kenneth," Her Majesty said.

"Not Miss Thompson what?" Boyd said. "What's going on anyhow?"

"She's reading my mind," Malone said.

"Well, then," Boyd snapped, "tell her to keep it to herself." The car started up again with a roar and Malone and the others were thrown around again, this time toward the back. There was a chorus of groans and squeals, and they were on their way once more.

"To reply to your question, Sir Kenneth," the Queen said.

Lady Barbara said, with some composure: "What question—Your Majesty?"

The Queen nodded regally at her. "Sir Kenneth was wondering why I wished to go to the Golden Palace," she said. "And my reply is this: it is none of your business why I want to go there. After all, is my word law, or isn't it?"

There didn't seem to be a good enough answer to that, Malone thought sadly. He kept quiet and was relieved to note that the others did the same. However, after a second he thought of something else.

"Your Majesty," he began carefully, "we've got to go to Yucca Flats tomorrow. Remember?"

"Certainly," the Queen said. "My memory is quite good, thank you. But that is tomorrow morning. We have the rest of the night left. It's only a little after nine, you know."

"Heavens," Barbara said. "Is it that late?"

"It's even later," Boyd said sourly. "It's much later than you think."

"And it's getting later all the time," Malone added.

"Pretty soon the sun will go out and all life on earth will end. Won't that be nice and peaceful?"

"I'm looking forward to it," Boyd said.

"I'm not," Barbara said. "But I've got to get some sleep tonight, if I'm going to be any good at all tomorrow."

You're pretty good right now, Malone thought, but he didn't say a word. He felt the Queen's eye on him but didn't turn around. After all, she was on his side—wasn't she?

At any rate, she didn't say anything.

"Perhaps it would be best," Barbara said, "if you and I—Your Majesty—just went home and rested up. Some other time, then, when there's nothing vital to do, we could—"

"No," the Queen said. "We couldn't. Really, Lady Barbara, how often will I have to remind you of the duties you owe your sovereign—not the least of which is obedience, as dear old Ben used to say."

"Ben?" Malone said, and immediately wished he hadn't.

"Johnson, dear boy," the Queen said. "Really a remarkable man—and such a good friend to poor Will. Why, did you ever hear the story of how he actually paid Will's rent in London once upon a time? That was while Will and that Anne of his were having one of their arguments, of course. I didn't tell you that story, did I?"

"No," Malone said truthfully, but his voice was full of foreboding. "If I might remind Your Majesty of the subject," he added tentatively, "I should like to say—"

"Remind me of the subject!" the Queen said, obviously delighted. "What a lovely pun! And how much better because purely unconscious! My, my, Sir Kenneth, I never suspected you of a pointed sense of humor—could you be a descendant of Sir Richard Greene, I wonder?"

"I doubt it," Malone said. "My ancestors were all poor but Irish." He paused. "Or, if you prefer, Irish, but poor." Another pause, and then he added: "If that means anything at all. Which I doubt."

"In any case," the Queen said, her eyes twinkling, "you were about to enter a new objection to our little visit to the Palace, were you not?"

Malone admitted as much. "I really think that—"

Her eyes grew suddenly cold. "If I hear any more objections, Sir Kenneth, I shall not only rescind your knighthood and—when I regain my rightful kingdom—deny you your dukedom, but I shall refuse to cooperate any further in the business of Project Isle."

Malone turned cold. His face, he knew without glancing in the mirror, was white and pale. He thought of what Burris would do to him if he didn't follow through on his assigned job.

Even if he wasn't as good as Burris thought he was, he really liked being an FBI agent. He didn't want to be fired.

And Burris had said: *"Give her anything she wants."*

He gulped and tried to make his face look normal. "All right," he said. "Fine. We'll go to the Palace."

He tried to ignore the pall of apprehension that fell over the car.

6

The management of the Golden Palace had been in business for many long, dreary, profitable years, and each member of the staff thought he or she had seen just about everything there was to be seen. And those that were new felt an obligation to *look* as if they'd seen everything.

Therefore, when the entourage of Queen Elizabeth I strolled into the main salon, not a single eye was batted. Not a single gasp was heard.

Nevertheless, the staff kept a discreet eye on the crew. Drunks, rich men or Arabian millionaires were all familiar. But a group out of the Sixteenth Century was something else again.

Malone almost strutted, conscious of the sidelong glances the group was drawing. But it was obvious that Sir Thomas was the major attraction. Even if you could accept the idea of people in strange costumes, the sight of a living, breathing absolute duplicate of King Henry VIII was a little too much to take. It has been reported that two ladies named Jane, and one named Catherine, came down with sudden headaches and left the salon within five minutes of the group's arrival.

Malone felt he knew, however, why he wasn't drawing his full share of attention. He felt a little out of place. The costume was one thing, and, to tell the truth, he was beginning to enjoy it. Even with the weight of the stuff, it was going to be a wrench to go back to single-breasted suits and plain white shirts. But he did feel that he should have been carrying a sword.

Instead, he had a .44 Magnum Colt snuggled beneath his left armpit.

Somehow, a .44 Magnum Colt didn't seem as romantic as a sword. Malone pictured himself saying: "Take that, varlet." Was varlet what you called them, he wondered. Maybe it was valet.

"Take that, valet," he muttered. No, that sounded even worse. Oh, well, he could look it up later.

The truth was that he had been born in the wrong century. He could imagine himself at the Mermaid Tavern, hob-nobbing with Shakespeare and all the rest of them. He wondered if Richard Greene would be there. Then he wondered who Richard Greene was.

Behind Sir Kenneth, Sir Thomas Boyd strode, looking majestic, as if he were about to fling purses of gold to the citizenry. As a matter of fact, Malone thought, he was. They all were.

Purses of good old United States of America gold.

Behind Sir Thomas came Queen Elizabeth and her Lady-in-Waiting, Lady Barbara Wilson. They made a beautiful foursome.

"The roulette table," Her Majesty said with dignity. "Precede me."

They pushed their way through the crowd. Most of the customers were either excited enough, drunk enough, or both to see nothing in the least incongruous about a Royal Family of the Tudors invading the Golden Palace. Very few of them, as a matter of fact, seemed to notice the group.

They were roulette players. They noticed nothing but the table and the wheel. Malone wondered what they were thinking about, decided to ask Queen Elizabeth, and then decided against it. He felt it would make him nervous to know.

Her Majesty took a handful of chips.

The handful was worth, Malone knew, exactly five thousand dollars. That, he'd thought, ought to last them an evening, even in the Golden Palace. In the center of the strip, inside the city limits of Las Vegas itself, the five thousand would have lasted much longer—but Her Majesty wanted the Palace, and the Palace it was.

Malone began to smile. Since he couldn't avoid the evening, he was determined to enjoy it. It was sort of fun, in its way, indulging a sweet harmless old lady. And there was nothing they could do until the next morning, anyhow.

His indulgent smile faded very suddenly.

Her Majesty plunked the entire handful of chips—*five thousand dollars!* Malone thought dazedly—onto the table. "Five thousand," she said in clear, cool measured tones, "on number one."

The croupier blinked only slightly. He bowed. "Yes, Your Majesty," he said.

Malone was briefly thankful, in the midst of his black horror, that he had called the management and told them that the Queen's plays were backed by the United States Government. Her Majesty was going to get unlimited credit—and a good deal of awed and somewhat puzzled respect.

Malone watched the spin begin with mixed feelings. There was five thousand dollars riding on the little ball. But, after all, Her Majesty was a telepath. Did that mean anything?

He hadn't decided by the time the wheel stopped, and by then he didn't have to decide.

"Thirty-four," the croupier said tonelessly. "Red, Even and High."

He raked in the chips with a nonchalant air.

Malone felt as if he had swallowed his stomach. Boyd and Lady Barbara, standing nearby, had absolutely no expressions on their faces. Malone needed no telepath to tell him what they were thinking.

They were exactly the same as he was. They were incapable of thought.

But Her Majesty never batted an eyelash. "Come, Sir Kenneth," she said. "Let's go on to the poker tables."

She swept out. Her entourage followed her, shambling a little, and blank-eyed. Malone was still thinking about the five thousand dollars. Oh, well, Burris had said to give the lady anything she wanted. *But my God!* he thought. *Did she have to play for royal stakes?*

"I am, after all, a Queen," she whispered back to him.

Malone thought about the National Debt. He wondered if a million more or less would make any real difference. There would be questions asked in committees about it. He tried to imagine himself explaining the evening to a group of Congressmen. "Well, you see, gentlemen, there was this roulette wheel—"

He gave it up.

Then he wondered how much hotter the water was going to get, and he stopped thinking altogether in self-defense.

In the next room, there were scattered tables. At one, a poker game was in full swing. Only five were playing; one, by his white-tie-and-tails uniform, was easily recognizable as a house dealer. The other four were all men, one of them in full cowboy regalia. The Tudors descended upon them with great suddenness, and the house dealer looked up and almost lost his cigarette.

"We haven't any money, Your Majesty," Malone whispered.

She smiled up at him sweetly, and then drew him aside. "If you were a telepath," she said, "how would *you* play poker?"

Malone thought about that for a minute, and then turned to look for Boyd. But Sir Thomas didn't even have to be given instructions. "Another five hundred?" he said.

Her Majesty sniffed audibly. "Another five thousand," she said regally.

Boyd looked Malonewards. Malone looked defeated. Boyd turned with a small sigh and headed for the cashier's booth. Three minutes later, he was back with a fat fistful of chips.

"Five grand?" Malone whispered to him.

"Ten," Boyd said. "I know when to back a winner."

Her Majesty went over to the table. The dealer had regained control, but looked up at them with a puzzled stare.

"You know," the Queen said, with an obvious attempt to put the man at his ease, "I've always wanted to visit a gambling hall."

"Sure, lady," the dealer said. "Naturally."

"May I sit down?"

The dealer looked at the group. "How about your friends?" he said cautiously.

The queen shook her head. "They would rather watch, I'm sure."

For once Malone blessed the woman's telepathic talent. He, Boyd and Barbara Wilson formed a kind of Guard of Honor around the chair which Her Majesty occupied. Boyd handed over the new pile of chips, and was favored with a royal smile.

"This is a poker game, ma'am," the dealer said to her quietly.

"I know, I know," Her Majesty said with a trace of testiness. "Roll 'em."

The dealer stared at her popeyed. Next to her, the gentleman in the cowboy outfit turned. "Ma'am, are you from around these parts?" he said.

"Oh, no," the Queen said. "I'm from England."

"England?" The cowboy looked puzzzled. "You don't seem to have any accent, ma'am," he said at last.

"Certainly not," the Queen said. "I've lost that; I've been over here a great many years."

Malone hoped fervently that Her Majesty wouldn't mention just how many years. He didn't think he could stand it, and he was almost grateful for the cowboy's nasal twang.

"Oil?" he said.

"Oh, no," Her Majesty said. "The Government is providing this money."

"The Government?"

"Certainly," Her Majesty said. "The FBI, you know."

There was a long silence.

At last, the dealer said: "Five-card draw your game, ma'am?"

"If you please," Her Majesty said.

The dealer shrugged and, apparently, commended his soul to a gambler's God. He passed the pasteboards around the table with the air of one who will have nothing more to do with the world.

Her Majesty picked up her hand.

"The ante's ten, ma'am," the dealer said softly.

Without looking, Her Majesty removed a ten-dollar chip from the pile before her and sent it spinning to the middle of the table.

The dealer opened his mouth, but said nothing. Malone, meanwhile, was peering over the Queen's shoulder.

She held a pair of nines, a four, a three and a Jack.

The man to the left of the dealer announced glumly: "Can't open."

The next man grinned. "Open for twenty," he said.

Malone closed his eyes. He heard the cowboy say: "I'm in," and he opened his eyes again. The Queen was pushing two ten-dollar chips toward the center of the table.

The next man dropped, and the dealer looked round the table. "How many?"

The man who couldn't open took three cards. The man who'd opened for twenty stood pat. Malone shuddered invisibly. That, he figured, meant a straight or better. And Queen Elizabeth Thompson was going in against at least a straight with a pair of nines, Jack high.

For the first time, it was borne in on Malone that being a telepath did not necessarily mean that you were a good poker player. Even if you knew what every other person at the table held, you could still make a whole lot of stupid mistakes.

He looked nervously at Queen Elizabeth, but her face was serene. Apparently she'd been following the thoughts of the poker players, and not concentrating on him at all. That was a relief. He felt, for the first time in days, as if he could think freely.

The cowboy said: "Two," and took them. It was Her Majesty's turn.

"I'll take two," she said, and threw away the three and four. It left her with the nine of spades and the nine of hearts, and the Jack of diamonds.

These were joined, in a matter of seconds, by two bright new cards: the six of clubs and the three of hearts.

Malone closed his eyes. *Oh, well,* he thought.

It was only thirty bucks down the drain. Practically nothing.

Of course Her Majesty dropped at once; knowing what the other players held, she knew she couldn't beat them after the draw. But she did like to take long chances, Malone thought miserably. Imagine trying to fill a full house on one pair!

Slowly, as the minutes passed, the pile of chips before Her Majesty dwindled. Once Malone saw her win with two pair against a reckless man trying to fill a straight on the other side of the table. But whatever was going on, Her Majesty's face was as calm as if she were asleep.

Malone's worked overtime. If the Queen hadn't been losing so obviously, the dealer might have mistaken the play of naked emotion across his visage for a series of particularly obvious signals.

An hour went by. Barbara left to find a ladies' lounge where she could sit down and try to relax. Fascinated in a horrible sort of way, both Malone and Boyd stood, rooted to the spot, while hand after hand went by and the ten thousand dollars dwindled to half that, to a quarter, and even less. . . .

Her Majesty, it seemed, was a damn poor poker player.

The ante had been raised by this time. Her Majesty was losing one hundred dollars a hand, even before the betting began. But she showed not the slightest indication to stop.

"We've got to get up in the morning," Malone announced to no one in particular, when he thought he couldn't possibly stand another half-hour of the game.

"So we do," Her Majesty said with a little regretful sigh. "Very well, then. Just one more hand."

"It's a shame to lose you," the cowboy said to her, quite sincerely. He had been winning steadily ever since Her Majesty sat down, and Malone thought that the man should, by this time, be awfully grateful to the United States Government. Somehow, he doubted that this gratitude existed.

Malone wondered if she should be allowed to stay for one more hand. There was, he estimated, about two thousand dollars in front of her. Then he wondered how he was going to stop her.

The cards were dealt.

The first man said quietly: "Open for two hundred."

Malone looked at the Queen's hand. It contained the Ace, King, Queen and ten of clubs—and the seven of spades.

Oh, no. He thought. *She couldn't possibly be thinking of filling a flush.*

He knew perfectly well that she was.

The second man said: "And raise two hundred."

The Queen equably tossed (counting, Malone thought, the ante) five hundred into the pot.

The cowboy muttered to himself for a second, and finally shoved in his money.

"I think I'll raise it another five hundred," the Queen said calmly.

Malone wanted to die of shock. Unfortunately, he remained alive and watching. He saw the last man, after some debate internal, shove a total of one thousand dollars into the pot.

"Cards?" said the dealer.

The first man said: "One."

It was too much to hope for, Malone thought. If that first man were trying to fill a straight or a flush, maybe he wouldn't make it. And maybe something final would happen to all the other players. But that was the only way he could see for Her Majesty to win.

The card was dealt. The second man stood pat and Malone's green tinge became obvious to the veriest dunce. The cowboy, on Her Majesty's right, asked for a card, received it and sat back without a trace of expression.

The Queen said: "I'll try one for size." She'd picked up poker lingo, and the basic rules of the game, Malone realized, from the other players—or possibly from someone at the hospital itself, years ago.

He wished she'd picked up something less dangerous instead, like a love of big-game hunting, or stunt-flying.

But no. It had to be poker.

The Queen threw away her seven of spades, showing more sense than Malone had given her credit for at any time during the game. She let the other card fall and didn't look at it.

She smiled up at Malone and Boyd. "Live dangerously," she said gaily.

Malone gave her a hollow laugh.

The last man drew one card, too, and the betting began.

The Queen's remaining thousand was gone before an eye could notice it. She turned to Boyd.

"Sir Thomas," she said. "Another five thousand, please. At once."

Boyd said nothing at all, but marched off. Malone noticed, however, that his step was neither as springy nor as confident as it had been before. For himself, Malone was sure that he could not walk at all.

Maybe, he thought hopefully, the floor would open up and swallow them all. He tried to imagine explaining the loss of $20,000 to Burris and some congressmen, and after that he watched the floor narrowly, hoping for the smallest hint of a crack in the palazzo marble.

"May I raise the whole five thousand?" the Queen said.

"It's okay with me," the dealer said. "How about the rest of you?"

The four grunts he got expressed a suppressed eagerness. The Queen took the new chips Boyd had brought her and shoved them into the center of the table with a fine, careless gesture of her hand. She smiled gaily at everybody. "Seeing me?" she said.

Everybody was.

"Well, you see, it was this way," Malone muttered to himself, rehearsing. He half-thought that one of the others would raise again, but no one did. After all, each of them must be convinced that he held a great hand, and though raising had gone on throughout the hand, each must now be afraid of going the least little bit too far and scaring the others out.

"Mr. Congressman," Malone muttered. "There's this game called poker. You play it with cards and money. Chiefly money."

That wasn't any good.

"You've been called," the dealer said to the first man, who'd opened the hand a year or so before.

"Why, sure," the player said, and laid down a pair of aces, a pair of threes—and a four. One of the threes, and the four, were clubs. That reduced the already improbable chances of the Queen's coming up with a flush.

"Sorry," said the second man, and laid down a straight with a single gesture. The straight was nine-high and there were no clubs in it. Malone felt devoutly thankful for that.

The second man reached for the money but, under the popeyed gaze of the dealer, the fifth man laid down another straight—this one ten high. The nine was a club Malone felt the odds go down, right in his own stomach.

And now the cowboy put down his cards. The King of diamonds. The King of hearts. The Jack of diamonds. The Jack of spades. And—the Jack of hearts.

Full house. "Well," said the cowboy, "I suppose that does it."

The Queen said: "Please. One moment."

The cowboy stopped halfway in his reach for the enormous pile of chips. The Queen laid down her four clubs—Ace, King, Queen and ten—and for the first time flipped over her fifth card.

It was the Jack of clubs.

"My God," the cowboy said, and it sounded like a prayer. "A royal flush."

"Naturally," the Queen said. "What else?"

Her Majesty calmly scooped up the tremendous pile of chips. The cowboy's hands fell away. Five mouths were open around the table.

Her Majesty stood up. She smiled sweetly at the men around the table. "Thank you very much, gentlemen," she said. She handed the chips to Malone, who took them in nerveless fingers. "Sir Kenneth," she said, "I hereby appoint you temporary Chancellor of the Exchequer—at least until Parliament convenes."

There was, Malone thought, at least thirty-five thousand dollars in the pile. He could think of nothing to say.

So, instead of using up words, he went and cashed in the chips. For once, he realized, the Government had made money on an investment. It was probably the first time since 1775.

Malone thought vaguely that the government ought to make more investments like the one he was cashing in. If it did, the National Debt could be wiped out in a matter of days.

He brought the money back. Boyd and the Queen were waiting for him, but Barbara was still in the ladies' lounge. "She's on the way out," the Queen informed him, and, sure enough, in a minute they saw the figure approaching them. Malone smiled at her, and, tentatively, she smiled back. They began the long march to the exit of the club, slowly and regally, though not by choice.

The crowd, it seemed, wouldn't let them go. Malone never found out, then or later, how the news of Her Majesty's winnings had gone through the place so fast, but everyone seemed to know about it. The Queen was the recipient of several low bows and a few drunken curtsies, and, when they reached the front door at last, the doorman said in a most respectful tone: "Good evening, Your Majesty."

The Queen positivley beamed at him. So, to his own great surprise, did Sir Kenneth Malone.

Outside, it was about four in the morning. They climbed into the car and headed back toward the hotel.

Malone was the first to speak. "How did you know that was a Jack of clubs?" he said in a strangled sort of voice.

The little old lady said calmly: "He was cheating."

"The dealer?" Malone asked.

The little old lady nodded.

"In *your* favor?"

"He couldn't have been cheating," Boyd said at the same instant. "Why would he want to give you all that money?"

The little old lady shook her head. "He didn't want to give it to me," she said. "He wanted to give it to the man in the cowboy's suit. His name is Elliott, by the way—Bernard L. Elliott. And he comes from Weehawken. But he pretends to be a Westerner so nobody will be suspicious of him. He and the dealer are in cahoots—isn't that the word?"

"Yes, Your Majesty," Boyd said. "That's the word." His tone was awed and respectful, and the little old lady gave a nod and became Queen Elizabeth I once more.

"Well," she said, "the dealer and Mr. Elliott were in cahoots, and the dealer wanted to give the hand to Mr. Elliott. But he made a mistake, and dealt the Jack of clubs to me. I watched him, and, of course, I knew what he was thinking. The rest was easy."

"My God," Malone said. "Easy."

Barbara said: "Did she win?"

"She won," Malone said with what he felt was positively magnificent understatement.

"Good," Barbara said, and lost interest at once.

Malone had seen the lights of a car in the rear-view mirror a few minutes before. When he looked now, the lights were still there—but the fact just didn't register until, a couple of blocks later, the car began to pull around them on the left. It was a Buick, while Boyd's was a new Lincoln, but the edge wasn't too apparent yet.

Malone spotted the gun barrel protruding from the Buick and yelled just before the first shot went off.

Boyd, at the wheel, didn't even bother to look. His reflexes took over and he slammed his foot down on the brake. The specially-built FBI Lincoln slowed down instantly. The shotgun blast splattered the glass of the curved windshield all over—but none of it came into the car itself.

Malone already had his hand on the butt of the .44 Magnum under his left armpit, and he even had time to be grateful, for once, that it wasn't a smallsword. The women were in the back seat, frozen, and he yelled: "Duck, damn it, duck!" and felt, rather than saw, both of them sink down onto the floor of the car.

The Buick had slowed down, too, and the gun barrel was swivelling back for a second shot. Malone felt naked and unprotected. The Buick and the Lincoln were even on the road now.

Malone had his revolver out. He fired the first shot without even realizing fully that he'd done so, and he heard a piercing scream from Barbara in the back seat. He had no time to look back.

A .44 Magnum is not, by any means, a small gun. As handguns go—revolvers and automatics—it is about as large as a gun can get to be. An ordinary car has absolutely no chance against it.

Much less the glass in an ordinary car.

The first slug drilled its way through the window glass as though it were not there, and slammed its way through an even more unprotected obstacle, the frontal bones of the triggerman's skull. The second slug from Malone's gun followed it right away, and missed the hole the first slug had made by something less than an inch.

The big, apelike thug who was holding the shotgun had a chance to pull the trigger once more, but he wasn't aiming very well. The blast merely scored the paint off the top of the Lincoln.

The rear window of the Buick was open, and Malone caught sight of another glint of blued steel from the corner of his eye. There was no time to shift aim—not with bullets flying like swallows on the way to Capistrano. Malone thought faster than he had imagined himself capable of doing, and decided to aim for the driver.

Evidently the man in the rear seat of the Buick had

had the same inspiration. Malone blasted two more high-velocity lead slugs at the driver of the big Buick, and at the same time the man in the Buick's rear seat fired at Boyd.

But Boyd had shifted tactics. He'd hit the brakes. Now he came down hard on the accelerator instead.

The chorus of shrieks from the Lincoln's back seat increased slightly in volume. Barbara, Malone knew, wasn't badly hurt; she hadn't even stopped for breath since the first shot had been fired. Anybody who could scream like that, he told himself, had to be healthy.

As the Lincoln leaped ahead, Malone pulled the trigger of his .44 twice more. The heavy, high-speed chunks of streamlined copper-coated lead leaped from the muzzle of the gun and slammed into the driver of the Buick without wasting any time. The Buick slewed across the highway.

The two shots fired by the man in the back seat went past Malone's head with a *whizz*, missing both him and Boyd by a margin too narrow to think about.

But those were the last shots. The only difference between the FBI and the Enemy seemed to be determination and practice.

The Buick spun into a flat sideskid, swivelled on its wheels and slammed into the ditch at the side of the road, turning over and over, making a horrible noise, as it broke up.

Boyd slowed the car again, just as there was a sudden blast of fire. The Buick had burst into flame and was spitting heat and smoke and fire in all directions. Malone sent one more bullet after it in a last flurry of action —saving his last one for possible later emergencies.

Boyd jammed on the brakes and the Lincoln came to a screaming halt. In silence he and Malone watched the burning Buick roll over and over into the desert beyond the shoulder.

"My God," Boyd said. "My ears!"

Malone understood at once. The blast from his own still-smoking .44 had roared past Boyd's head during the gun battle. No wonder the man's ears hurt. It was a wonder he wasn't altogether deaf.

But Boyd shook off the pain and brought out his own .44 as he stepped out of the car. Malone followed him, his gun trained.

From the rear, Her Majesty said: "It's safe to rise now, isn't it?"

"You ought to know," Malone said. "You can tell if they're still alive."

There was silence while Queen Elizabeth frowned for a moment in concentration. A look of pain crossed her face, and then, as her expression smoothed again, she said: "The traitors are dead. All except one, and he's—" She paused. "He's dying," she finished. "He can't hurt you."

There was no need for further battle. Malone reholstered his .44 and turned to Boyd. "Tom, call the State Police," he said. "Get 'em down here fast."

He waited while Boyd climbed back under the wheel and began punching buttons on the dashboard. Then Malone went toward the burning Buick.

He tried to drag the men out, but it wasn't any use. The first two, in the front seat, had the kind of holes in them people talked about throwing elephants through. Head and chest had been hit.

Malone couldn't get close enough to the fiercely blazing automobile to make even a try for the men in the back seat.

He was sitting quietly on the edge of the rear seat when the Nevada Highway Patrol cars drove up next to them. Barbara Wilson had stopped screaming, but she was still sobbing on Malone's shoulder. "It's all right," he told her, feeling ineffectual.

"I never saw anybody killed before," she said.

"It's all right," Malone said. "Nothing's going to hurt you. I'll protect you."

He wondered if he meant it, and found, to his surprise, that he did. Barbara Wilson sniffled and looked up at him. "Mr. Malone—"

"Ken," he said.

"I'm sorry," she said. "Ken—I'm so afraid. I saw the

hole in one of the men's heads, when you fired—it was—"

"Don't think about it," Malone said. To him, the job had been an unpleasant occurrence, but a job, that was all. He could see, though, how it might affect people who were new to it.

"You're so brave," she said.

Malone tightened his arm around the girl's shoulder. "Just depend on me," he said. "You'll be all right if you—"

The State Trooper walked up then, and looked at them. "Mr. Malone?" he said. He seemed to be taken slightly aback at the costuming.

"That's right," Malone said. He pulled out his ID card and the little golden badge. The State Patrolman looked at them, and looked back at Malone.

"What's with the getup?" he said.

"FBI," Malone said, hoping his voice carried conviction. "Official business."

"In costume?"

"Never mind about the details," Malone snapped.

"He's an FBI agent, sir," Barbara said.

"And what are you?" the Patrolman said. "Lady Jane Grey?"

"I'm a nurse," Barbara said. "A psychiatric nurse."

"For nuts?"

"For disturbed patients."

The Patrolman thought that over. "Hell, you've got the identity cards and stuff," he said at last. "Maybe you've got a reason to dress up. How would I know? I'm only a State Patrolman."

"Let's cut the monologue," Malone said savagely, "and get to business."

The Patrolman stared. Then he said: "All right, sir. Yes, sir. I'm Lieutenant Adams, Mr. Malone. Suppose you tell me what happened?"

Carefully and concisely, Malone told him the story of the Buick that had pulled up beside them, and what happened afterward.

Meanwhile, the other cops had been looking over the wreck. When Malone had finished his story, Lieutenant Adams flipped his notebook shut and looked over toward them. "I guess it's okay, sir," he said. "As far as I'm concerned, it's justifiable homicide. Self-defense. Any reason why they'd want to kill you?"

Malone thought about the Golden Palace. That might be a reason—but it might not. And why burden an innocent State Patrolman with the facts of FBI life?

"Official," he said. "Your chief will get the report."

The Patrolman nodded. "I'll have to take a deposition tomorrow, but—"

"I know," Malone said. "Thanks. Can we go on to our hotel now?"

"I guess," the Patrolman said. "Go ahead. We'll take care of the rest of this. You'll be getting a call later."

"Fine," Malone said. "Trace those hoods, and any connections they might have had. Get the information to me as soon as possible."

Lieutenant Adams nodded. "You won't have to leave the state, will you?" he asked. "I don't mean that you *can't,* exactly—hell, you're FBI. But it'd be easier—"

"Call Burris in Washington," Malone said. "He can get hold of me—and if the Governor wants to know where we are, or the State's Attorney, put them in touch with Burris too. Okay?"

"Okay," Lieutenant Adams said. "Sure." He blinked at Malone. "Listen," he said. "About those costumes—"

"We're trying to catch Henry VIII for the murder of Anne Boleyn," Malone said with a polite smile. "Okay?"

"I was only asking," Lieutenant Adams said. "Can't blame a man for asking, now, can you?"

Malone climbed into his front seat. "Call me later," he said. The car started. "Back to the hotel, Sir Thomas," Malone said, and the car roared off.

7

Yucca Flats, Malone thought, certainly deserved its name. It was about as flat as land could get, and it contained millions upon millions of useless yuccas. Perhaps they were good for something, Malone thought, but they weren't good for *him*.

The place might, of course, have been called Cactus Flats, but the cacti were neither as big nor as impressive as the yuccas.

Or was that yucci?

Possibly, Malone mused, it was simply yucks.

And whatever it was, there were millions of it. Malone

felt he couldn't stand the sight of another yucca. He was grateful for only one thing.

It wasn't summer. If the Elizabethans had been forced to drive in closed cars through the Nevada desert in the summertime, they might have started a cult of nudity, Malone felt. It was bad enough now, in what was supposed to be winter.

The sun was certainly bright enough, for one thing. It glared through the cloudless sky and glanced with blinding force off the road. Sir Thomas Boyd squinted at it through the rather incongruous sunglasses he was wearing, while Malone wondered idly if it was the sunglasses, or the rest of the world, that was an anachronism. But Sir Thomas kept his eyes grimly on the road as he gunned the powerful Lincoln toward the Yucca Flats Labs at eighty miles an hour.

Malone twisted himself around and faced the women in the back seat. Past them, through the rear window of the Lincoln, he could see the second car. It followed them gamely, carrying the newest addition to Sir Kenneth Malone's Collection of Bats.

"Bats?" Her Majesty said suddenly, but gently. "Shame on you, Sir Kenneth. These are poor, sick people. We must do our best to help them—not to think up silly names for them. For shame!"

"I suppose so," Malone said wearily. He sighed and, for the fifth time that day, he asked: "Does Your Majesty have any idea where our spy is now?"

"Well, really, Sir Kenneth," the Queen said with the slightest of hesitations, "it isn't easy, you know. Telepathy has certain laws, just like everything else. After all, even a game has laws. Being telepathic didn't help me to play poker—I still had to learn the rules. And telepathy has rules, too. A telepath can easily confuse another telepath by using some of those rules."

"Oh, fine," Malone said. "Well, have you got into contact with his mind yet?"

"Oh, yes," Her Majesty said happily. "And my goodness, he's certainly digging up a lot of information, isn't he?"

Malone moaned softly. "But who *is* he?" he asked after a second.

The Queen stared at the roof of the car in what looked like concentration. "He hasn't thought of his name yet," she said. "I mean, at least, if he has, he hasn't mentioned it to me. Really, Sir Kenneth, you have no idea how difficult all this is."

Malone swallowed with difficulty. *"Where* is he, then," said. "Can you tell me that, at least? His location?"

Her Majesty looked positively desolated with sadness. "I can't be sure," she said. "I really can't be exactly sure just where he is. He does keep moving around, I know that. But you have to remember that he doesn't want me to find him. He certainly doesn't want to be found by the FBI—would you?"

"Your Majesty," Malone said, "I *am* the FBI."

"Yes," the Queen said, "but suppose you weren't? He's doing his best to hide himself, even from me. It's sort of a game he's playing."

"A game!"

Her Majesty looked contrite. "Believe me, Sir Kenneth, the minute I know exactly where he is, I'll tell you. I promise. Cross my heart and hope to die—which I can't, of course, being immortal." Nevertheless, she made an X-mark over her left breast. "All right?"

"All right," Malone said, out of sheer necessity. "Okay. But don't waste any time telling me. Do it right away. We've *got* to find that spy and isolate him somehow."

"Please don't worry yourself, Sir Kenneth," Her Majesty said. "Your Queen is doing everything she can."

"I know that, Your Majesty," Malone said. "I'm sure of it." Privately, he wondered just how much even she could do. Then he realized—for perhaps the ten-thousandth time—that there was no such thing as wondering privately any more.

"That's quite right, Sir Kenneth," the Queen said sweetly. "And it's about time you got used to it."

"What's going on?" Boyd said. "More reading minds back there?"

"That's right, Sir Thomas," the Queen said.

"I've about gotten used to it," Boyd said almost cheerfully. "Pretty soon they'll come and take me away, but I don't mind at all." He whipped the car around a bend in the road savagely. "Pretty soon they'll put me with the other sane people and let the bats inherit the world. But I don't mind at all."

"Sir Thomas!" Her Majesty said in shocked tones.

"Please," Boyd said with a deceptive calmness. "Just Mr. Boyd. Not even Lieutenant Boyd, or Sergeant Boyd. Just Mr. Boyd. Or, if you prefer, Tom."

"Sir Thomas," Her Majesty said, "I really can't understand this sudden—"

"Then don't understand it," Boyd said. "All I know is everybody's nuts, and I'm sick and tired ot it."

A pall of silence fell over the company.

"Look, Tom," Malone began at last.

"Don't you try smoothing me down," Boyd snapped. Malone's eyebrows rose. "Okay," he said. "I won't smooth you down. I'll just tell you to shut up, to keep driving—and to show some respect to Her Majesty."

"I—" Boyd stopped. There was a second of silence.

"That's better," Her Majesty said with satisfaction.

Lady Barbara stretched in the back seat, next to Her Majesty. "This is certainly a long drive," she said. "Have we got much farther to go?"

"Not too far," Malone said. "We ought to be there soon."

"I—I'm sorry for the way I acted," Barbara said.

"What do you mean, the way you acted?"

"Crying like that," Barbara said with some hesitation. "Making an—absolute idiot of myself. When that other car —tried to get us."

"Don't worry about it," Malone said. "It was nothing."

"I just—made trouble for you," Barbara said.

Her Majesty touched the girl on the shoulder. "He's not thinking about the trouble you cause him," she said quietly.

"Of course I'm not," Malone told her.

"But I—"

"My dear girl," Her Majesty said, "I believe that Sir Kenneth is, at least partly, in love with you."

Malone blinked. It was perfectly true—even if he

hadn't quite known it himself until now. Telepaths, he was discovering, were occasionally handy things to have around.

"In . . . love . . ." Barbara said.

"And you, my dear—" Her Majesty began.

"Please, Your Majesty," Lady Barbara said. "No more. Not just now."

The Queen smiled, almost to herself. "Certainly, dear," she said.

The car sped on. In the distance, Malone could see the blot on the desert that indicated the broad expanse of Yucca Flats Labs. Just the fact that it could be seen, he knew, didn't mean an awful lot. Malone had been able to see it for the past fifteen minutes, and it didn't look as if they'd gained an inch on it. Desert distances are deceptive.

At long last, however, the main gate of the laboratories hove into view. Boyd made a left turn off the highway and drove a full seven miles along the restricted road, right up to the big gate that marked the entrance of the laboratories themselves. Once again, they were faced with the army of suspicious guards and security officers.

This time, suspicion was somewhat heightened by the dress of the visitors. Malone had to explain about six times that the costumes were part of an FBI arrangement, that he had not stolen his identity cards, that Boyd's cards were Boyd's, too, and in general that the four of them were not insane, not spies, and not jokesters out for a lark in the sunshine.

Malone had expected all of that. He went through the rigamarole wearily but without any sense of surprise. The one thing he hadn't been expecting was the man who was waiting for him on the other side of the gate.

When he'd finished identifying everybody for the fifth or sixth time, he began to climb back into the car. A familiar voice stopped him cold.

"Just a minute, Malone," Andrew J. Burris said. He erupted from the guardhouse like an avenging angel, followed closely by a thin man, about five feet ten inches in height, with brush-cut brown hair, round horn-rimmed spectacles, large hands and a small Sir Francis Drake beard. Malone looked at the two figures blankly.

"Something wrong, Chief?" he said.

Burris came toward the car. The thin gentleman followed him, walking with an odd bouncing step that must have been acquired, Malone thought, over years of treading on rubber eggs. "I don't know," Burris said when he'd reached the door. "When I was in Washington, I seemed to know—but when I get out here in this desert, everything just goes haywire." He rubbed at his forehead.

Then he looked into the car. "Hello, Boyd," he said pleasantly.

"Hello, Chief," Boyd said.

Burris blinked. "Boyd, you look like Henry VIII," he said with only the faintest trace of surprise.

"Doesn't he, though?" Her Majesty said from the rear seat. "I've noticed that resemblance myself."

Burris gave her a tiny smile. "Oh," he said. "Hello, Your Majesty. I'm—"

"Andrew J. Burris, Director of the FBI," the Queen finished for him. "Yes, I know. It's very nice to meet you at last. I've seen you on television, and over the video phone. You photograph badly, you know."

"I do?" Burris said pleasantly. It was obvious that he was keeping himself under very tight control.

Malone felt remotely sorry for the man—but only remotely. Burris might as well know, he thought, what they had all been going through the past several days.

Her Majesty was saying something about the honorable estate of knighthood, and the Queen's list. Malone began paying attention when she came to: "—and I hereby dub thee—" She stopped suddenly, turned and said: "Sir Kenneth, give me your weapon."

Malone hesitated for a long, long second. But Burris' eye was on him, and he could interpret the look without much trouble. There was only one thing for him to do. He pulled out his .44, ejected the cartridges in his palm (and reminded himself to reload the gun as soon as he got it back), and handed the weapon to the Queen, butt foremost.

She took the butt of the revolver in her right hand,

leaned out the window of the car, and said in a fine, distinct voice: "Kneel, Andrew."

Malone watched with wide, astonished eyes as Andrew J. Burris, Director of the FBI, went to one knee in a low and solemn genuflection. Queen Elizabeth Thompson nodded her satisfaction.

She tapped Burris gently on each shoulder with the muzzle of the gun. "I knight thee Sir Andrew," she said. She cleared her throat. "My, this desert air is dry . . . Rise, Sir Andrew, and know that you are henceforth Knight Commander of the Queen's Own FBI."

"Thank you, Your Majesty," Burris said humbly.

He rose to his feet silently. The Queen withdrew into the car again and handed the gun back to Malone. He thumbed the cartridges into the chambers of the cylinder and listened dumbly.

"Your Majesty," Burris said, "this is Dr. Harry Gamble, the head of Project Isle. Dr. Gamble, this is Her Majesty the Queen; Lady Barbara Wilson, her—uh—her lady-in-waiting; Sir Kenneth Malone; and King—I mean Sir Thomas Boyd." He gave the four a single bright impartial smile. Then he tore his eyes away from the others, and bent his gaze on Sir Kenneth Malone. "Come over here a minute, Malone," he said, jerking his thumb over his shoulder. "I want to talk to you."

Malone climbed out of the car and went around to meet Burris. He felt just a little worried as he followed the Director away from the car. True, he had sent Burris a long telegram the night before, in code. But he hadn't expected the man to show up in Yucca Flats. There didn't seem to be any reason for it.

And when there isn't any reason, Malone told himself sagely, it's a bad one.

"What's the trouble, Chief?" he asked.

Burris sighed. "None so far," he said quietly. "I got a report from the Nevada State Patrol, and ran it through R&I. They identified the men you killed, all right—but it didn't do us any good. They're hired hoods."

"Who hired them?" Malone said.

Burris shrugged. "Somebody with money," he said. "Hell, men like that would kill their own grandmothers if the price were right—you know that. We can't trace them back any farther."

Malone nodded. That was, he had to admit, bad news. But then, when had he last had any good news?

"We're nowhere near our telepathic spy," Burris said. "We haven't come any closer than we were when we started. Have you got anything? Anything at all, no matter how small?"

"Not that I know of, sir," Malone said.

"What about the little old lady—what's her name? Thompson. Anything from her?"

Malone hesitated. "She has a close fix on the spy, sir," he said slowly, "but she doesn't seem able to identify him right away."

"What else does she want?" Burris said. "We've made her Queen and given her a full retinue in costume; we've let her play roulette and poker with Government money. Does she want to hold a mass execution? If she does, I can supply some Congressmen, Malone. I'm sure it could be arranged." He looked at the agent narrowly. "I might even be able to suppply an FBI man or two," he added.

Malone swallowed hard. "I'm trying the best I can, sir," he said. "What about the others?"

Burris looked even unhappier than usual. "Come along," he said. "I'll show you."

When they got back to the car, Dr. Gamble was talking spiritedly with Her Majesty about Roger Bacon. "Before my time, of course," the Queen was saying, "but I'm sure he was a most interesting man. Now when dear old Marlowe wrote his *Faust,* he and I had several long discussions about such matters. Alchemy, Doctor—"

Burris interrupted with: "I beg your pardon, Your Majesty, but we must get on. Perhaps you'll be able to continue your—ah—audience later." He turned to Boyd. "Sir Thomas," he said with an effort, "drive directly to the Westinghouse buildings. Over that way." He pointed. "Dr. Gamble will ride with you, and the rest of us will follow in the second car. Let's move."

He stepped back as the project head got into the car, and watched it roar off. Then he and Malone went to the second car, another FBI Lincoln. Two agents were sitting in the back seat, with a still figure between them.

With a shock, Malone recognzied William Logan and the agents he'd detailed to watch the telepath. Logan's face did not seem to have changed expression since Malone had seen it last, and he wondered wildly if perhaps it had to be dusted once a week.

He got in behind the wheel and Burris slid in next to him.

"Westinghouse," Burris said. "And let's get there in a hurry."

"Right," Malone said, and started the car.

"We just haven't had a single lead," Burris said. "I was hoping you'd come up with something. Your telegram detailed the fight, of course, and the rest of what's been happening—but I hoped there'd be something more."

"There isn't," Malone was forced to admit. "All we can do is try to persuade Her Majesty to tell us—"

"Oh, I know it isn't easy," Burris said. "But it seems to me . . ."

By the time they'd arrived at the administrative offices of Westinghouse's psionics research area, Malone found himself wishing that something would happen. Possibly, he thought, lightning might strike, or an earthquake swallow everything up. He was, suddenly, profoundly tired of the entire affair.

8

Four days later, he was more than tired. He was exhausted. The six psychopaths—including Her Majesty Queen Elizabeth I—had been housed in a converted dormitory in the Westinghouse area, together with four highly nervous and even more highly trained and investigated psychiatrists from St. Elizabeths in Washington. The Convention of Nuts, as Malone called it privately, was in full swing.

And it was every bit as strange as he'd thought it was going to be. Unfortunately, five of the six (Her Majesty being the only exception) were completely out of contact with the world. The psychiatrists referred to them in worried tones as "unavailable for therapy," and spent most of their time brooding over possible ways of bringing them back into the real world for a while, at least far enough so that they could be spoken with.

Malone stayed away from the five who were completely psychotic. The weird babblings of fifty-year-old Barry Miles disconcerted him. They sounded like little Charlie O'Neill's strange semi-connected jabber, but Westinghouse's Dr. O'Connor said that it seemed to represent another pheomenon entirely. William Logan's blank face was a memory of horror, but the constant tinkling giggles of Ardith Parker, the studied and concentrated way that Gordon Macklin wove meaningless patterns in the air with his waving fingers, and the rhythmless, melodyless humming that seemed to be all there was to the personality of Robert Cassiday were simply too much for Malone. Taken singly, each was frightening and remote; all together, they wove a picture of insanity that chilled him more than he wanted to admit.

When the seventh telepath was flown in from Honolulu, Malone didn't even bother to see her. He let the psychiatrists take over directly, and simply avoided their sessions.

Queen Elizabeth I, on the other hand, he found genuinely likeable. According to the psych boys, she had been (as both Malone and Her Majesty had theorized) heavily frustrated by being the possessor of a talent which no one else recognized. Beyond that, the impact of other minds was disturbing; there was a slight loss of identity which seemed to be a major factor in every case of telepathic insanity. But the Queen had compensated for her frustrations in the easiest possible way; she had simply traded her identity for another one, and had rationalized a single, overruling delusion: that she was Queen Elizabeth I of England, still alive and wrongfully deprived of her throne.

"It's a beautiful rationalization," one of the psychiatrists said with more than a trace of admiration in his voice. "Complete and thoroughly consistent. She's just traded identities—and everything else she does—*everything* else—stems logically out of her delusional premise. Beautiful."

She may have been crazy, Malone realized. But she was a long way from stupid.

The project was in full swing. The only trouble was that they were no nearer finding the telepath than they had been three weeks before. With five completely blank human beings to work with, and the sixth Queen Elizabeth (Malone heard privately that the last telepath, the girl from Honolulu, was no better than the first five; she had apparently regressed into what one of the psychiatrists called a "non-identity childhood syndrome." Malone didn't know what it meant, but it sounded terrible.)—with that crew, Malone could see why progress was their most difficult commodity.

Dr. Harry Gamble, the head of Project Isle, was losing poundage by the hour with worry. And, Malone reflected, he could ill afford it.

Burris, Malone and Boyd had set themselves up in a temporary office within the Westinghouse area. The Director had left his assistant in charge in Washington. Nothing, he said over and over again, was as important as the spy in Project Isle.

Apparently Boyd had come to believe that, too. At any rate, though he was still truculent, there were no more outbursts of rebellion.

But, on the fourth day:

"What do we do now?" Burris asked.

"Shoot ourselves," Boyd said promptly.

"Now, look here—" Malone began, but he was overruled.

"Boyd," Burris said levelly, "if I hear any more of that sort of pessimism, you're going to be an exception to the beard rule. One more crack out of you, and you can go out and buy yourself a razor."

Boyd put his hand over his chin protectively, and said nothing at all.

"Wait a minute," Malone said. "Aren't there any *sane* telepaths in the world?"

"We can't find any," Burris said. "We—"

There was a knock at the office door.

"Who's there?" Burris called.

"Dr. Gamble," said the man's surprisingly baritone voice.

Burris called: "Come in, Doctor," and the door opened. Dr. Gamble's lean face looked almost haggard.

"Mr. Burris," he said, extending his arms a trifle, "can't anything be done?" Malone had seen Gamble speaking before, and had wondered if it would be possible for the man to talk with his hands tied behind his back. Apparently it wouldn't be. "We feel that we are approaching a critical stage in Project Isle," the scientist said, enclosing one fist within the other hand. "If anything more gets out to the Soviets, we might as well publish our findings—" a wide, outflung gesture of both arms—"in the newspapers."

Burris stepped back. "We're doing the best we can, Dr. Gamble," he said. All things considered, his obvious try at radiating confidence was nearly successful. "After all," he went on, "we know a great deal more than we did four days ago. Miss Thompson has assured us that the spy is right here, within the compound of Yucca Flats Labs. We've bottled everything up in this compound, and I'm confident that no information is at present getting through to the Soviet Government. Miss Thompson agrees with me."

"Miss Thompson?" Gamble said, one hand at his bearded chin.

"The Queen," Burris said.

Gamble nodded and two fingers touched his forehead. "Ah," he said. "Of course." He rubbed at the back of his neck. "But we can't keep everybody who's here now locked up forever. Sooner or later we'll have to let them—" His left hand described the gesture of a man tossing away a wad of paper—"go." His hands fell to his sides. "We're lost, unless we can find that spy."

"We'll find him," Burris said with a show of great confidence.

"But—"

"Give her time," Burris said. "Give her time. Remember her mental condition."

Boyd looked up. "Rome," he said in an absent fashion, "wasn't built in a daze."

Burris glared at him, but said nothing. Malone filled the conversational hole with what he thought would be nice, and hopeful, and untrue.

"We know he's someone on the reservation, so we'll catch him eventually," he said. "And as long as his information isn't getting into Soviet hands, we're safe." He glanced at his wristwatch.

Dr. Gamble said: "But—"

"My, my," Malone said. "Almost lunchtime. I have to go over and have lunch with Her Majesty. Maybe she's dug up something more."

"I hope so," Dr. Gamble said, apparently successfully deflected. "I do hope so."

"Well," Malone said, "pardon me." He shucked off his coat and trousers. Then he proceeded to put on the doublet and hose that hung in the little office closet. He shrugged into the fur-trimmed, slash-sleeved coat, adjusted the plumed hat to his satisfaction with great care, and gave Burris and the others a small bow. "I go to an audience with Her Majesty, gentlemen," he said in a grave, well-modulated voice. "I shall return anon."

He went out the door and closed it carefully behind him. When he had gone a few steps he allowed himself the luxury of a deep sigh.

Then he went outside and across the dusty street to the barracks where Her Majesty and the other telepaths were housed. No one paid any attention to him, and he rather missed the stares he'd become used to drawing. But by now, everybody was used to seeing Elizabethan clothing. Her Majesty had arrived at a new plateau.

She would now allow no one to have audience with her unless he was properly dressed. Even the psychiatrists—whom she had, with a careful sense of meiosis, appointed Physicians to the Royal House—had to wear the stuff.

Malone went over the whole case in his mind—for about the thousandth time, he told himself bitterly.

Who could the telepathic spy be? It was like looking

for a needle in a rolling stone, he thought. Or something. He did remember clearly that a stitch in time saved nine, but he didn't know nine what, and suspected it had nothing to do with his present problem.

How about Dr. Harry Gamble, Malone thought. It seemed a little unlikely that the head of Project Isle would be spying on his own men—particularly since he already had all the information. But, on the other hand, he was just as probable a spy as anybody else.

Malone moved onward. Dr. Thomas O'Connor, the Westinghouse psionics man, was the next nominee. Before Malone had actually found Her Majesty, he had had a suspicion that O'Connor had cooked the whole thing up to throw the FBI off the trail and confuse everybody, and that he'd intended merely to have the FBI chase ghosts while the real spy did his work undetected.

But what if O'Connor were the spy himself—a telepath? What if he were so confident of his ability to throw the Queen off the track that he had allowed the FBI to find all the other telepaths? There was another argument for that: he'd had to report the findings of his machine no matter what it cost him; there were too many other men on his staff who knew about it.

O'Connor was a perfectly plausible spy, too. But he didn't seem very likely. The head of a government project is likely to be a much-investigated man. Could any tie-up with Russia—even a psionic one—stand up against that kind of investigation? It was possible. Anything, after all, was possible. You eliminated the impossible, and then whatever remained, however improbable . . .

Malone told himself morosely to shut up and think.

O'Connor, he told himself, might be the spy. It would be a pleasure, he realized, to go to the office of that superior scientist and arrest him. "I know your true name," he muttered. "It isn't O'Connor, it's Moriarty." He wondered if the Westinghouse man had ever done any work on the dynamics of an asteroid. Then he wondered what the dynamics of an asteroid were.

But if O'Connor were the spy, nothing made sense.

Why would he have disclosed the fact that people were having their minds read in the first place?

Sadly, Malone gave up the idea.

But, then, there were other ideas.

The other psychiatrists, for instance...

The only trouble with them, Malone realized, was that there seemed to be neither motive nor anything else to connect them to the case. There was no evidence, none in any direction.

Why, there was just as much evidence that the spy was really Kenneth J. Malone, he told himself. And then he stopped.

Maybe Tom Boyd had been thinking that way about him. Maybe Boyd suspected that he, Malone, was really the spy.

Certainly it worked in reverse. Boyd...

No, Malone told himself firmly. That was silly.

If he were going to consider Boyd, he realized, he might as well go whole hog and think about Andrew J. Burris.

And that really *was* ridiculous. Absolutely ridic...

Well, Queen Elizabeth had seemed pretty certain when she'd pointed him out in Dr. Dowson's office. And the fact that she'd apparently changed her mind didn't have to mean very much. After all, how much faith could you place in Her Majesty at the best of times? If she'd made a mistake about Burris in the first place, she could just as well have made a mistake in the second place. Or about the spy's being at Yucca Flats at all.

In which case, Malone thought sadly, they were right back where they'd started from.

Behind their own goal line.

One way or another, though, Her Majesty had made a mistake. She'd pointed Burris out as the spy, and then she'd said she'd been wrong. Either Burris was a spy, or else he wasn't. You couldn't have it both ways.

And if Burris really were the spy, Malone thought, then why had he started the investigation in the first place? You came back to the same question with Burris, he realized, that you had with Dr. O'Connor: it didn't make sense for a man to play one hand against the other.

Maybe the right hand sometimes didn't know what the left hand was doing, but this was ridiculous.

So Burris wasn't the spy. And Her Majesty had made a mistake when she'd said . . .

"Wait a minute," Malone told himself suddenly.

Had she?

Maybe, after all, you *could* have it both ways. The thought occurred to him with a startling suddenness and he stood silent upon a peak in Yucca Flats, contemplating it. A second went by.

And then something Burris himself had said came back to him, something that—

"I'll be damned," he muttered.

He came to a dead stop in the middle of the street. In one sudden flash of insight, all the pieces of the case he'd been looking at for so long fell together and formed one consistent picture. The pattern was complete.

Malone blinked.

In that second, he knew exactly who the spy was.

A jeep honked raucously and swerved around him. The driver leaned out to curse and Malone waved at him, dimly recognizing a private eye he had once known, a middle-aged man named Archer. Wondering vaguely what Archer was doing this far East, and in a jeep at that, Malone watched the vehicle disappear down the street. There were more cars coming, but what difference did that make? Malone didn't care about cars. After all, he had the answer, the whole answer. . . .

"I'll be damned," he said again, abruptly, and wheeled around to head back to the offices.

On the way, he stopped in at another small office, this one inhabited by the two FBI men from Las Vegas. He gave a series of quick orders, and got the satisfaction, as he left, of seeing one of the FBI men grabbing for a phone in a hurry.

It was good to be *doing* things again, important things.

Burris, Boyd and Dr. Gamble were still talking as Malone entered.

"That," Burris said, "was one hell of a quick lunch. What's Her Majesty doing now—running a diner?"

Malone ignored the bait, and drew himself to his full

height. "Gentlemen," he said solemnly, "Her Majesty has asked that all of us attend her in audience. She has information of the utmost gravity to impart, and wishes this audience at once."

Dr. Gamble made a puzzled, circular gesture with one hand. "What's the matter?" he asked. "Is something—" The hand dropped—"wrong?"

Burris barely glanced at him. A startled expression came over his features. "Has she—" he began, and stopped, leaving his mouth open and the rest of the sentence unfinished.

Malone nodded gravely and drew in a breath. Elizabethan periods were hard on the lungs, he had begun to realize: you needed a lot of air before you embarked on a sentence. "I believe, gentlemen," he said, "that Her Majesty is about to reveal the identity of the spy who has been battening on Project Isle."

The silence lasted no more than three seconds. Dr. Gamble didn't even make a gesture during that time. Then Burris spoke.

"Let's go," he snapped. He wheeled and headed for the door. The others promptly followed.

"Gentlemen!" Malone said, sounding, as far as he could tell, properly shocked and offended. "Your dress!"

"What?" Dr. Gamble said, throwing up both hands.

"Oh, *no*," Boyd chimed in. "Not now."

Burris simply said: "You're quite right. Get dressed, Boyd—I mean, of course, Sir Thomas."

While they were dressing, Malone put in a call to Dr. O'Connor's office. The scientist was as frosty as ever.

"Yes, Mr. Malone?" The sound of that voice, Malone reflected, was enough to give anybody double revolving pneumonia with knobs on.

"Dr. O'Connor," he said, "Her Majesty wants you in her court in ten minutes—and in full court dress."

O'Connor merely sighed, like Boreas. "What is this," he asked, "more tomfoolery?"

"I really couldn't say," Malone told him coyly. "But I'd advise you to be there. It might interest you."

"Interest me?" O'Connor stormed. "I've got work to

do here—important work. You simply do not realize, Mr. Malone—"

"Whatever I realize," Malone cut in, feeling brave, "I'm passing on orders from Her Majesty."

"That insane woman," O'Connor stated flatly, "is not going to order me about. Good Lord, do you know what you're saying?"

Malone nodded. "I certainly do," he said cheerfully. "If you'd rather, I can have the orders backed up by the United States Government. But that won't be necessary, will it?"

"The United States Government," O'Connor said, thawing perceptibly about the edges, "ought to allow a man to do his proper work, and not force him to go chasing off after the latest whims of some insane old lady."

"You will be there, now, won't you?" Malone asked. His own voice reminded him of something, and in a second he had it: the cooing, gentle persuasion of Dr. Andrew Blake of Rice Pavilion, who had locked Malone in a padded cell. It was the voice of a man talking to a mental case.

It sounded remarkably apt. Dr. O'Connor went slightly purple, but controlled himself magnificently. "I'll be there," he said.

"Good," Malone told him, and snapped the phone off.

Then he put in a second call to the psychiatrists from St. Elizabeths and told them the same thing. More used to the strange demands of neurotic and psychotic patients, they were readier to comply.

Everyone, Malone realized with satisfaction, was now assembling. Burris and the others were ready to go, sparklingly dressed and looking impatient. Malone put down the phone and took one great breath of relief.

Then, beaming, he led the others out.

Ten minutes later, there were nine men in Elizabethan costume standing outside the room which had been designated as the Queen's Court. Dr. Gamble's costume did not quite fit him; his sleeve-ruffs were half way up to his elbows and his doublet had an unfortunate tendency to creep. The St. Elizabeths men, all four of them, looked just a little like moth-eaten versions of old silent pictures. Malone looked them over with a somewhat sardonic eye. Not only did he have the answer to the whole problem that had been plaguing them, but *his* costume was a stunning, perfect fit.

"Now, I want you men to let me handle this," Malone said. "I know just what I want to say, and I think I can get the information without too much trouble."

One of the psychiatrists spoke up. "I trust you won't disturb the patient, Mr. Malone," he said.

"Sir Kenneth," Malone snapped.

The psychiatrist looked both abashed and worried. "I'm sorry," he said doubtfully.

Malone nodded. "That's all right," he said. "I'll try not to disturb Her Majesty unduly."

The psychiatrists conferred. When they came out of the huddle one of them—Malone was never able to tell them apart—said: "Very well, we'll let you handle it. But we will be forced to interfere if we feel you're—ah —going too far."

Malone said: "That's fair enough, gentlemen. Let's go."

He opened the door.

It was a magnificent room. The whole place had been done over in plastic and synthetic fibers to look like something out of the Sixteenth Century. It was as garish, and as perfect, as a Hollywood movie set—which wasn't surprising, since two stage designers had been hired away from color-TV spectaculars to set it up. At the far end of the room, past the rich hangings and the flaming chandeliers, was a great throne, and on it Her Majesty was seated. Lady Barbara reclined on the steps at her feet.

Malone saw the expression on Her Majesty's face. He wanted to talk to Barbara—but there wasn't time. Later, there might be. Now, he collected his mind and drove one thought at the Queen, one single powerful thought:

Read me! You know by this time that I have the truth— but read deeper!

The expression on her face changed suddenly. She was

smiling a sad, gentle little smile. Lady Barbara, who had looked up at the approach of Sir Kenneth and his entourage, relaxed again, but her eyes remained on Malone. "You may approach, my lords," said the Queen.

Sir Kenneth led the procession, with Sir Thomas and Sir Andrew close behind him. O'Connor and Gamble came next, and bringing up the rear were the four psychiatrists. They strode slowly along the red carpet that stretched from the door to the foot of the throne. They came to a halt a few feet from the steps leading up to the throne, and bowed in unison.

"You may explain, Sir Kenneth," Her Majesty said.

"Your Majesty understands the conditions?" Malone asked.

"Perfectly," said the Queen. "Proceed."

Now the expression on Barbara's face changed, to wonder and a kind of fright. Malone didn't look at her. Instead, he turned to Dr. O'Connor.

"Dr. O'Connor, what are your plans for the telepaths who have been brought here?" He shot the question out quickly, and O'Connor was caught off-balance.

"Well—ah—we would like their cooperation in further research which we—ah—plan to do into the actual mechanisms of telepathy. Provided, of course—" He coughed gently—"provided that they become—ah—accessible. Miss—I mean, of course, Her Majesty has already been a great deal of help." He gave Malone an odd look. It seemed to say: *What's coming next?*

Malone simply gave him a nod, and a "Thank you, Doctor," and turned to Burris. He could feel Barbara's eyes on him, but he went on with his prepared questions. "Chief," he said, "what about you? After we nail our spy, what happens—to Her Majesty, I mean? You don't intend to stop giving her the homage due her, do you?"

Burris stared, openmouthed. After a second he managed to say: "Why, no, of course not, Sir Kenneth. That is—" and he glanced over at the psychiatrists—"if the doctors think . . ."

There was another hurried consultation. The four psychiatrists came out of it with a somewhat shaky statement to the effect that treatments which had been proven to have some therapeutic value ought not to be discontinued, although of course there was always the chance that . . .

"Thank you, gentlemen," Malone said smoothly. He could see that they were nervous, and no wonder; he could imagine how difficult it was for a psychiatrist to talk about a patient in her presence. But they'd already realized that it didn't make any difference; their thoughts were an open book, anyway.

Lady Barbara said: "Sir—I mean Ken—are you going to—"

"What's this all about?" Burris snapped.

"Just a minute, Sir Andrew," Malone said. "I'd like to ask one of the doctors here—or all of them, for that matter—one more question." He whirled and faced them. "I'm assuming that not one of these persons is legally responsible for his or her actions. Is that correct?"

Another hurried huddle. The psych boys were beginning to remind Malone of a sem-pro football team in rather unusual uniforms.

Finally one of them said: "You are correct. According to the latest statutes, all of these persons are legally insane—including Her Majesty." He paused and gulped. "I except the FBI, of course—and ourselves." Another pause. "And Dr. O'Connor and Dr. Gamble."

"And," said Lady Barbara, "me." She smiled sweetly at them all.

"Ah," the psychiatrist said. "Certainly. Of course." He retired into his group with some confusion.

Malone was looking straight at the throne. Her Majesty's countenance was serene and unruffled.

Barbara said suddenly: "You don't mean—but she—" and closed her mouth. Malone shot her one quick look, and then turned to the Queen.

"Well, Your Majesty?" he said. "You have seen the thoughts of every man here. How do they appear to you?"

Her voice contained both tension and relief. "They are all good men, basically—and kind men," she said. "And they believe us. That's the important thing, you know. Their belief in us . . . Just as you said that first day

137

we met. We've needed belief for so long . . . for so long . . ." Her voice trailed off; it seemed to become lost in a constellation of thoughts. Barbara had turned to look up at Her Majesty.

Malone took a step forward, but Burris interrupted him. "How about the spy?" he said.

Then his eyes widened. Boyd, standing next to him, leaned suddenly forward. "That's why you mentioned all that about legal immunity because of insanity," he whispered. "Because—"

"No," Barbara said. "No. She couldn't—she's not—"

They were all looking at Her Majesty, now. She returned them stare for stare, her back stiff and straight and her white hair enhaloed in the room's light. "Sir Kenneth," she said—and her voice was only the least bit unsteady—"they all think *I'm* the spy."

Barbara stood up. "Listen," she said. "I didn't like Her Majesty at first—well, she was a patient, and that was all, and when she started putting on airs . . . but since I've gotten to know her I do like her. I like her because she's good and kind herself, and because—because she wouldn't be a spy. She couldn't be. No matter what any of you think—even you—Sir Kenneth!"

There was a second of silence.

"Of course she's not," Malone said quietly. "She's no spy."

"Would I spy on my own subjects?" she said. "Use your reason!"

"You mean—" Burris began, and Boyd finished for him:

"—she isn't?"

"No," Malone snapped. "She isn't. Remember, you said it would take a telepath to catch a telepath?"

"Well—" Burris began.

"Well, Her Majesty remembered it," Malone said. "And acted on it."

Barbara remained standing. She went to the Queen and put an arm around the little old lady's shoulder. Her Majesty did not object. "I knew," she said. "You couldn't have been a spy."

"Listen, dear," the Queen said. "Your Kenneth has seen the truth of the matter. Listen to him."

"Her Majesty not only caught the spy," Malone said, "but she turned the spy right over to us."

He turned at once and went back down the long red carpet to the door. *I really ought to get a sword,* he thought, and didn't see Her Majesty smile. He opened the door with a great flourish and said quietly: "Bring him in, boys."

The FBI men from Las Vegas marched in. Between them was their prisoner, a boy with a vacuous face, clad in a straitjacket that seemed to make no difference at all to him. His mind was—somewhere else. But his body was trapped between the FBI agents: the body of William Logan.

"Impossible," one of the psychiatrists said.

Malone spun on his heel and led the way back to the throne. Logan and his guards followed closely.

"Your Majesty," Malone said. "May I present the prisoner?"

"Perfectly correct, Sir Kenneth," the Queen said. "Poor Willie is your spy. You won't be too hard on him, will you?"

"I don't think so, Your Majesty," Malone said. "After all—"

"Now wait a minute," Burris exploded. "How the hell did *you* know any of this?"

Malone bowed to Her Majesty, and winked at Barbara. He turned to Burris. "Well," he said, "I had one piece of information none of the rest of you had. When we were in the Desert Edge Sanatorium, Dr. Dowson called you on the phone. Remember?"

"Sure I remember," Burris said. "So?"

"Well," Malone said, "Her Majesty said she knew just where the spy was. I asked her where—"

"Why didn't you tell me?" Burris screamed. "You knew all this time and you didn't tell me?"

"Hold on," Malone said. "I asked her where—and she said: 'He's right there.' And she was pointing right at your image on the screen."

Burris opened his mouth. Nothing came out. He

139

closed it and tried again. At last he managed one word.

"Me?" he said.

"You," Malone said. "But that's what I realized later. She wasn't pointing at you. She was pointing at Logan, who was in the next room."

Barbara whispered: "Is that right, Your Majesty?"

"Certainly, dear," the Queen said calmly. "Would I lie to Sir Kenneth?"

Malone was still talking. "The thing that set me off this noon was something you said, Sir Andrew," he went on. "You said there weren't any sane telepaths—remember?"

Burris, incapable of speech, merely nodded.

"But according to Her Majesty," Malone said, "we had every telepath in the United States right here. She told me that—and I didn't even see it!"

"Don't blame yourself, Sir Kenneth," the Queen put in. "I did do my best to mislead you, you know."

"You sure did!" Malone said. "And later on, when we were driving here, she said the spy was 'moving around.' That's right; he was in the car behind us, going eighty miles an hour."

Barbara stared. Malone got a lot of satisfaction out of that stare. But there was still more ground to cover.

"Then," he said, "she told us he was here at Yucca Flats—after we brought him here! It had to be one of the other six telepaths."

The psychiatrist who'd muttered: "Impossible," was still muttering it. Malone ignored him.

"And when I remembered her pointing at you," Malone told Burris, "and remembered that she'd only said: 'He's right there,' I knew it had to be Logan. You weren't there. You were only an image on a TV screen. Logan was there—in the room behind the phone."

Burris had found his tongue. "All right," he said. "Okay. But what's all this about misleading us—and why didn't she tell us right away, anyhow?"

Malone turned to Her Majesty on the throne. "I think that the Queen had better explain that—if she will."

Queen Elizabeth Thompson nodded very slowly. "I— I only wanted you to respect me," she said. "To treat me properly." Her voice sounded uneven, and her eyes were glistening with unspilled tears. Lady Barbara tightened her arm about the Queen's shoulders once more.

"It's all right," she said. "We do—respect you."

The Queen smiled up at her.

Malone waited. After a second Her Majesty continued.

"I was afraid that as soon as you found poor Willie you'd send me back to the hospital," she said. "And Willie couldn't tell the Russian agents any more once he'd been taken away. So I thought I'd just—just let things stay the way they were as long as I could. That's —that's all."

Malone nodded. After a second he said: "You see that we couldn't possibly send you back now, don't you?"

"I—"

"You know all the State Secrets, Your Majesty," Malone said. "We would rather that Dr. Harman in San Francisco didn't try to talk you out of them. Or anyone else."

The Queen smiled tremulously. "I know too much, do I?" she said. Then her grin faded. "Poor Dr. Harman," she said.

"Poor Dr. Harman?"

"You'll hear about him in a day or so," she said. "I—peeked inside his mind. He's very ill."

"Ill?" Lady Barbara asked.

"Oh, yes," the Queen said. The trace of a smile appeared on her face. "He thinks that all the patients in the hospital can see inside his mind."

"Oh, my," Lady Barbara said—and began to laugh. It was the nicest sound Malone had ever heard.

"Forget Harman," Burris snapped. "What about this spy ring? How was Logan getting his information out?"

"I've already taken care of that," Malone said. "I had Desert Edge Sanatorium surrounded as soon as I knew what the score was." He looked at one of the agents holding Logan.

"They ought to be in the Las Vegas jail within half an hour," he said in confirmation.

"Dr. Dowson was in on it, wasn't he, Your Majesty?" Malone said.

"Certainly," the Queen said. Her eyes were suddenly very cold. "I hope he tries to escape. I hope he tries it."

Malone knew just how she felt.

One of the psychiatrists spoke up suddenly. "I don't understand it," he said. "Logan is completely catatonic. Even if he could read minds, how could he tell Dowson what he'd read? It doesn't make sense."

"In the first place," the Queen said patiently, "Willie isn't catatonic. He's just *busy,* that's all. He's only a boy, and—well, he doesn't much like being who he is. So he visits other people's minds, and that way he becomes *them* for a while. You see?"

"Vaguely," Malone said. "But how did Dowson get his information? I had everything worked out but that."

"I know you did," the Queen said, "and I'm proud of you. I intend to award you with the Order of the Bath for this day's work."

Unaccountably, Malone's chest swelled with pride.

"As for Dr. Dowson," the Queen said, "that traitor—*hurt* Willie. If he's hurt enough, he'll come back." Her eyes weren't hard any more. "He didn't want to be a spy, really," she said, "but he's just a boy, and it must have sounded rather exciting. He knew that if he told Dowson everything he'd found out, they'd let him go—go away again."

There was a long silence.

"Well," Malone said, "that about wraps it up. Any questions?"

He looked around at the men, but before any of them could speak up Her Majesty rose.

"I'm sure there are questions," she said, "but I'm really very tired. My lords, you are excused." She extended a hand. "Come, Lady Barbara," she said. "I think I really may need that nap, now."

Malone put the cufflinks in his shirt with great care. They were great stones, and Malone thought that they gave his costume that necessary Elizabethan flair.

Not that he was wearing the costumes of the Queen's Court now. Instead, he was dressed in a tailor-proud suit of dark blue, a white-on-white shirt and no tie. He selected one of a gorgeous peacock pattern from his closet rack.

Boyd yawned at him from the bed in the room they were sharing. "Stepping out?" he said.

"I am," Malone said with restraint. He whipped the tie round his neck and drew it under the collar.

"Anybody I know?"

"I am meeting Lady Barbara, if you wish to know," Malone said.

"My God," Boyd said. "Come down. Relax. Anyhow, I've got a question for you. There was one little thing Her Everlovin' Majesty didn't explain."

"Yes?" said Malone.

"Well, about those hoods who tried to gun us down," Boyd said. "Who hired 'em? And why?"

"Dowson," Malone said. "He wanted to kill us off, and then kidnap Logan from the hotel room. But we foiled his plan—by killing his hoods. By the time he could work up something else, we were on our way to Yucca Flats."

"Great," Boyd said. "And how did you find out this startling piece of information? There haven't been any reports in from Las Vegas, have there?"

"No," Malone said.

"Okay," Boyd said. "I give up, Mastermind."

Malone wished Boyd would stop using that nickname. The fact was—as he, and apparently nobody else, was willing to recognize—that he wasn't anything like a really terrific FBI agent. Even Barbara thought he was something special.

He wasn't, he knew.

He was just lucky.

"Her Majesty informed me," Malone said.

"Her—" Boyd stood with his mouth dropped open, like a fish waiting for some bait. "You mean she knew?"

"Well," Malone said, "she did know the guys in the Buick weren't the best in the business—and she knew all about the specially-built FBI Lincoln. She got that from our minds." He knotted his tie with an air of great aplomb, and went slowly to the door. "And she knew we were a good team. She got that from our minds, too."

"But," Boyd said. After a second he said: "But," again, and followed it with: "Why didn't she tell us?"

Malone opened the door.

"Her Majesty wished to see the Queen's Own FBI in action," said Sir Kenneth Malone.

The End